PRAISE FOR FALLING MAN

'A revelatory piece of writing that will stand as a testament to
DeLillo's genius'
Times Literary Supplement

'He has been writing this book, or versions of it,
all through his career. The world seems to have been
catching up with DeLillo. His preoccupations – political
violence, dissociation, futurity, the mediated environment,
the fear of catastrophe – have been present from the off.
Falling Man . . . demands and rewards attention'
Sam Leith, *Spectator*

'The Nostradamus of contemporary fiction'
Sunday Herald

'DeLillo's precise, incantatory prose style and disjointed
dialogue captures the sense of a jolted city slowly trying to
rediscover normality . . . *Falling Man* engages with 9/11
on multiple levels: intellectual, emotional, artistic'
Financial Times

'Highly impressive, superbly eloquent'
David Sexton, *Evening Standard*

'As fine a thing as DeLillo has ever made . . . There are those
who have called him a cold writer, too detached, too cerebral;
I challenge them to read the astonishing and deeply moving
closing pages of *Falling Man* without weeping'
John Burnside, *Scotsman*

FALLING MAN

Don DeLillo is the author of fourteen novels,
including *White Noise* and *Libra*, and three plays.
He has won the National Book Award, the PEN/ Faulkner
Award and the Jerusalem Prize. In 2006, *Underworld* was
named one of the three best novels of the last twenty-five
years by the *New York Times Book Review* and in 2000 it
won the Howells Medal of the American Academy of
Arts and Letters for the most distinguished work
of fiction of the past five years.

DON DeLILLO

FALLING MAN

A NOVEL

PICADOR

First published 2007 by Scribner, New York

First published in Great Britain 2007 by Picador

First published in paperback 2007 by Picador

This edition first published 2012 by Picador
an imprint of Pan Macmillan, a division of Macmillan Publishers Limited
Pan Macmillan, 20 New Wharf Road, London N1 9RR
Basingstoke and Oxford
Associated companies throughout the world
www.panmacmillan.com

ISBN 978-1-4472-2437-2

A CIP catalogue record for this book is available from
the British Library.

Designed by Erich Hobbing
Printed and bound in the UK by
CPI Group (UK) Ltd, Croydon, CR0 4YY

FALLING MAN

PART ONE

BILL LAWTON

1

It was not a street anymore but a world, a time and space of falling ash and near night. He was walking north through rubble and mud and there were people running past holding towels to their faces or jackets over their heads. They had handkerchiefs pressed to their mouths. They had shoes in their hands, a woman with a shoe in each hand, running past him. They ran and fell, some of them, confused and ungainly, with debris coming down around them, and there were people taking shelter under cars.

The roar was still in the air, the buckling rumble of the fall. This was the world now. Smoke and ash came rolling down streets and turning corners, busting around corners, seismic tides of smoke, with office paper flashing past, standard sheets with cutting edge, skimming, whipping past, otherworldly things in the morning pall.

He wore a suit and carried a briefcase. There was glass in his hair and face, marbled bolls of blood and light. He walked past a Breakfast Special sign and they went running by, city cops and security guards running, hands pressed down on gun butts to keep the weapons steady.

Things inside were distant and still, where he was supposed to be. It happened everywhere around him, a car half buried in debris, windows smashed and noises coming out, radio voices scratching at the wreckage. He saw people shedding water as they ran, clothes and bodies drenched from sprinkler systems. There were shoes discarded in the street, handbags and laptops, a man seated on the sidewalk coughing up blood. Paper cups went bouncing oddly by.

The world was this as well, figures in windows a thousand feet up, dropping into free space, and the stink of fuel fire, and the steady rip of sirens in the air. The noise lay everywhere they ran, stratified sound collecting around them, and he walked away from it and into it at the same time.

There was something else then, outside all this, not belonging to this, aloft. He watched it coming down. A shirt came down out of the high smoke, a shirt lifted and drifting in the scant light and then falling again, down toward the river.

They ran and then they stopped, some of them, standing there swaying, trying to draw breath out of the burning air, and the fitful cries of disbelief, curses and lost shouts, and the paper massed in the air, contracts, resumés blowing by, intact snatches of business, quick in the wind.

He kept on walking. There were the runners who'd stopped and others veering into sidestreets. Some were walking backwards, looking into the core of it, all those writhing lives back there, and things kept falling, scorched objects trailing lines of fire.

He saw two women sobbing in their reverse march, looking past him, both in running shorts, faces in collapse.

He saw members of the tai chi group from the park nearby, standing with hands extended at roughly chest level, elbows bent, as if all of this, themselves included, might be placed in a state of abeyance.

Someone came out of a diner and tried to hand him a bottle of water. It was a woman wearing a dust mask and a baseball cap and she withdrew the bottle and twisted off the top and then thrust it toward him again. He put down the briefcase to take it, barely aware that he wasn't using his left arm, that he'd had to put down the briefcase before he could take the bottle. Three police vans came veering into the street and sped downtown, sirens sounding. He closed his eyes and drank, feeling the water pass into his body taking dust and soot down with it. She was looking at him. She said something he didn't hear and he handed back the bottle and picked up the briefcase. There was an after-taste of blood in the long draft of water.

He started walking again. A supermarket cart stood upright and empty. There was a woman behind it, facing him, with police tape wrapped around her head and face, yellow caution tape that marks the limits of a crime scene. Her eyes were thin white ripples in the bright mask and she gripped the handle of the cart and stood there, looking into the smoke.

In time he heard the sound of the second fall. He crossed Canal Street and began to see things, somehow, differently. Things did not seem charged in the usual ways, the cobbled street, the cast-iron buildings. There was something critically missing from the things around him. They were unfinished, whatever that means. They were unseen, whatever that means, shop windows, loading platforms, paint-sprayed walls. Maybe this is what things look like when there is no one here to see them.

He heard the sound of the second fall, or felt it in the trem-bling air, the north tower coming down, a soft awe of voices in the distance. That was him coming down, the north tower.

The sky was lighter here and he could breathe more easily. There were others behind him, thousands, filling the middle dis-tance, a mass in near formation, people walking out of the smoke. He kept going until he had to stop. It hit him quickly, the knowledge that he couldn't go any farther.

He tried to tell himself he was alive but the idea was too obscure to take hold. There were no taxis and little traffic of any kind and then an old panel truck appeared, Electrical Contractor, Long Island City, and it pulled alongside and the driver leaned toward the window on the passenger's side and examined what he saw, a man scaled in ash, in pulverized matter, and asked him where he wanted to go. It wasn't until he got in the truck and shut the door that he understood where he'd been going all along.

2

It wasn't just those days and nights in bed. Sex was everywhere at first, in words, phrases, half gestures, the simplest intimation of altered space. She'd put down a book or magazine and a small pause settled around them. This was sex. They'd walk down a street together and see themselves in a dusty window. A flight of stairs was sex, the way she moved close to the wall with him just behind, to touch or not, brush lightly or press tight, feeling him crowd her from below, his hand moving around her thigh, stopping her, the way he eased up and around, the way she gripped his wrist. The tilt she gave her sunglasses when she turned and looked at him or the movie on TV when the woman comes into the empty room and it doesn't matter whether she picks up the phone or takes off her skirt as long as she's alone and they are watching. The rented beach house was sex, entering at night after the long stiff drive, her body feeling welded at the joints, and she'd hear the soft heave of surf on the other side of the dunes, the thud and run, and this was the line of separation, the sound out there in the dark that marked an earthly pulse in the blood.

She sat thinking about this. Her mind drifted in and out of this, the early times, eight years ago, of the eventual extended grimness called their marriage. The day's mail was in her lap.

There were matters to attend to and there were events that crowded out such matters but she was looking past the lamp into the wall, where they seemed to be projected, the man and woman, bodies incomplete but bright and real.

It was the postcard that snapped her back, on top of the cluster of bills and other mail. She glanced at the message, a standard scrawled greeting, sent by a friend staying in Rome, then looked again at the face of the card. It was a reproduction of the cover of Shelley's poem in twelve cantos, first edition, called *Revolt of Islam*. Even in postcard format, it was clear that the cover was beautifully designed, with a large illustrated *R* that included creatural flourishes, a ram's head and what may have been a fanciful fish with a tusk and a trunk. *Revolt of Islam*. The card was from the Keats-Shelley House in Piazza di Spagna and she'd understood in the first taut seconds that the card had been sent a week or two earlier. It was a matter of simple coincidence, or not so simple, that a card might arrive at this particular time bearing the title of that specific book.

This was all, a lost moment on the Friday of that lifelong week, three days after the planes.

She said to her mother, "It was not possible, up from the dead, there he was in the doorway. It's so lucky Justin was here with you. Because it would have been awful for him to see his father like that. Like gray soot head to toe, I don't know, like smoke, standing there, with blood on his face and clothes."

"We did a puzzle, an animal puzzle, horses in a field."

Her mother's apartment was not far from Fifth Avenue, with art on the walls, painstakingly spaced, and small bronze pieces on tables and bookshelves. Today the living room was in a state of happy disarray. Justin's toys and games were scattered across the floor, subverting the timeless quality of the room, and this was nice, Lianne thought, because it was otherwise hard not to whisper in such a setting.

"I didn't know what to do. I mean with the phones out. Finally we walked to the hospital. Walked, step by step, like walking a child."

"Why was he there in the first place, in your apartment?"

"I don't know."

"Why didn't he go straight to a hospital? Down there, downtown. Why didn't he go to a friend's place?"

Friend meant girlfriend, an unavoidable thrust, she had to do it, couldn't help it.

"I don't know."

"You haven't discussed this. Where is he now?"

"He's all right. Done with doctors for a while."

"What have you discussed?"

"No major problems, physical."

"What have you discussed?" she said.

Her mother, Nina Bartos, had taught at universities in California and New York, retiring two years earlier, the So-and-So Professor of Such-and-Such, as Keith said once. She was pale and thin, her mother, following knee-replacement surgery. She was finally and resolutely old. This is what she wanted, it seemed, to be old and tired, to embrace old age, take up old age, surround herself with it. There were the canes, there were the medications, there were the afternoon naps, the dietary restrictions, the doctors' appointments.

"There's nothing to discuss right now. He needs to stay away from things, including discussions."

"Reticent."

"You know Keith."

"I've always admired that about him. He gives the impression there's something deeper than hiking and skiing, or playing cards. But what?"

"Rock climbing. Don't forget."

"And you went with him. I did forget."

Her mother stirred in the chair, feet propped on the matching stool, late morning, still in her robe, dying for a cigarette.

"I like his reticence, or whatever it is," she said. "But be careful."

"He's reticent around you, or was, the few times there was actual communication."

"Be careful. He was in grave danger, I know. He had friends in there. I know that too," her mother said. "But if you let your sympathy and goodwill affect your judgment."

There were the conversations with friends and former colleagues about knee replacements, hip replacements, about the atrocities of short-term memory and long-term health insurance. All of this was so alien to Lianne's sense of her mother that she thought there might be an element of performance. Nina was trying to accommodate the true encroachments of age by making drama of them, giving herself a certain degree of ironic distance.

"And Justin. Having a father around the house again."

"The kid is fine. Who knows how the kid is? He's fine, he's back in school," she said. "They reopened."

"But you worry. I know this. You like to nourish your fear."

"What's next? Don't you ask yourself? Not only next month. Years to come."

"Nothing is next. There is no next. This was next. Eight years ago they planted a bomb in one of the towers. Nobody said what's next. This was next. The time to be afraid is when there's no reason to be afraid. Too late now."

Lianne stood by the window.

"But when the towers fell."

"I know."

"When this happened."

"I know."

"I thought he was dead."

"So did I," Nina said. "So many watching."

"Thinking he's dead, she's dead."

"I know."

"Watching those buildings fall."

"First one, then the other. I know," her mother said.

She had several canes to choose from and sometimes, on the off-hours and the rainy days, she walked up the street to the Metropolitan Museum and looked at pictures. She looked at three or four pictures in an hour and a half of looking. She looked at what was unfailing. She liked the big rooms, the old masters, what was unfailing in its grip on the eye and mind, on memory and identity. Then she came home and read. She read and slept.

"Of course the child is a blessing but otherwise, you know better than I, marrying the man was a huge mistake, and you willed it, you went looking for it. You wanted to live a certain way, never mind the consequences. You wanted a certain thing and you thought Keith."

"What did I want?"

"You thought Keith would get you there."

"What did I want?"

"To feel dangerously alive. This was a quality you associated with your father. But that wasn't the case. Your father was at heart a careful man. And your son is a beautiful and sensitive child," she said. "But otherwise."

In truth she loved this room, Lianne did, in its most composed form, without the games and scattered toys. Her mother had been living here for a few years only and Lianne tended to see it as a visitor might, a space that was serenely self-possessed, and so what if it's a little intimidating. What she loved most were the two still lifes on the north wall, by Giorgio Morandi, a painter her mother had studied and written about. These were groupings of bottles, jugs, biscuit tins, that was all, but there was something in the brushstrokes that held a mystery she could not name, or in the irregular edges of vases and jars, some reconnoiter inward, human and obscure, away from the very light and color of the paintings. *Natura morta.* The Italian term for still life seemed stronger than it had to be, somewhat ominous, even, but these were matters she hadn't talked about with her mother. Let the latent meanings turn and bend in the wind, free from authoritative comment.

"You liked asking questions as a child. Insistently digging. But you were curious about the wrong things."

"They were my things, not yours."

"Keith wanted a woman who'd regret what she did with him. This is his style, to get a woman to do something she'll be sorry for. And the thing you did wasn't just a night or a weekend. He was built for weekends. The thing you did."

"This isn't the time."

"You actually married the man."

"And then I threw him out. I had strong objections, building up over time. What you object to is very different. He's not a scholar, not an artist. Doesn't paint, doesn't write poetry. If he did, you'd overlook everything else. He'd be the raging artist. He'd be allowed to behave unspeakably. Tell me something."

"You have more to lose this time. Self-respect. Think about that."

"Tell me this. What kind of painter is allowed to behave more unspeakably, figurative or abstract?"

She heard the buzzer and walked over to the intercom to listen to the doorman's announcement. She knew what it was in advance. This would be Martin on the way up, her mother's lover.

3

He signed a document, then another. There were people on gurneys and there were others, a few, in wheelchairs, and he had trouble writing his name and more trouble fastening the hospital gown behind him. Lianne was there to help. Then she wasn't anymore and an orderly put him in a wheelchair and pushed him down a corridor and into a series of examining rooms, with urgent cases rolling by.

Doctors in scrubs and paper masks checked his airway and took blood-pressure readings. They were interested in potentially fatal reactions to injury, hemorrhage, dehydration. They looked for diminished blood flow to tissues. They studied the contusions on his body and peered into his eyes and ears. Someone gave him an EKG. Through the open door he saw IV racks go floating past. They tested his hand grip and took X rays. They told him things he could not absorb about a ligament or cartilage, a tear or sprain.

Someone took the glass out of his face. The man talked throughout, using an instrument he called a pickup to extract small fragments of glass that were not deeply embedded. He said that most of the worst cases were in hospitals downtown or at the trauma center on a pier. He said that survivors were not appearing in the numbers expected. He was propelled by events and could not stop talking. Doctors and volunteers were standing idle, he said, because the people they were waiting for were mostly back there, in the ruins. He said he would use a clamp for deeper fragments.

"Where there are suicide bombings. Maybe you don't want to hear this."

"I don't know."

"In those places where it happens, the survivors, the people nearby who are injured, sometimes, months later, they develop bumps, for lack of a better term, and it turns out this is caused by small fragments, tiny fragments of the suicide bomber's body. The bomber is blown to bits, literally bits and pieces, and fragments of flesh and bone come flying outward with such force and velocity that they get wedged, they get trapped in the body of anyone who's in striking range. Do you believe it? A student is sitting in a café. She survives the attack. Then, months later, they find these little, like, pellets of flesh, human flesh that got driven into the skin. They call this organic shrapnel."

He tweezered another splinter of glass out of Keith's face.

"This is something I don't think you have," he said.

Justin's two best friends were a sister and brother who lived in a high-rise ten blocks away. Lianne had trouble remembering their names at first and called them the Siblings and soon the name stuck. Justin said this was their real name anyway and she thought what a funny kid when he wants to be.

She saw Isabel on the street, mother of the Siblings, and they stood at the corner talking.

"That's what kids do, absolutely, but I have to admit I'm beginning to wonder."

"They sort of conspire."

"Yes, and sort of talk in code, and they spend a lot of time at the window in Katie's room, with the door closed."

"You know they're at the window."

"Because I can hear them talking when I walk by and I know that's where they're standing. They're at the window talking in this sort of code. Maybe Justin tells you things."

"I don't think so."

"Because it's getting a little strange, frankly, all the time they spend, first, sort of huddled together, and then, I don't know, like endlessly whispering things in this semi-gibberish, which is what kids do, absolutely, but still."

Lianne wasn't sure what this was all about. It was about three kids being kids together.

"Justin's getting interested in the weather. I think they're doing clouds in school," she said, realizing how hollow this sounded.

"They're not whispering about clouds."

"Okay."

"It has something to do with this man."

"What man?"

"This name. You've heard it."

"This name," Lianne said.

"Isn't this the name they sort of mumble back and forth? My kids totally don't want to discuss the matter. Katie enforces the thing. She basically inspires fear in her brother. I thought maybe you would know something."

"I don't think so."

"Like Justin says nothing about any of this?"

"No. What man?"

"What man? Exactly," Isabel said.

He was tall, with cropped hair, and she thought he looked like army, like career military, still in shape and beginning to look seasoned, not in combat but in the pale rigors of this life, in separation perhaps, in living alone, being a father from a distance.

He was in bed now and watched her, a few feet away, begin to button her shirt. They slept in the same bed because she could not tell him to use the sofa and because she liked having him here next to her. He didn't seem to sleep. He lay on his back and talked but mostly listened and this was all right. She didn't need to know a man's feelings about everything, not anymore and not this man. She liked the spaces he made. She liked dressing in front of him. She knew the time was coming when he'd press her to the wall before she finished dressing. He'd get out of bed and look at her and she'd stop what she was doing and wait for him to come and press her to the wall.

He lay on a long narrow table within the closed unit. There was a pillow under his knees and a pair of track lights overhead and he tried to listen to the music. Inside the powerful noise of the scanner he fixed his attention on the instruments, separating one set from another, strings, woodwinds, brass. The noise was a violent staccato knocking, a metallic clamor that made him feel he was deep inside the core of a science-fiction city about to come undone.

He wore a device on his wrist to produce a detailed image and the sense of helpless confinement made him think of something the radiologist had said, a Russian whose accent he found reassuring because these are serious people who place weight on every word and maybe that's why he chose classical music to listen to when she asked him to make a selection. He heard her now in his headset saying that the next sequence of noise would last three minutes and when the music resumed he thought of Nancy Dinnerstein, who ran a sleep clinic in Boston. People paid her to put them to sleep. Or the other Nancy, what's-her-name, briefly, between incidental sex acts, in Portland that time, Oregon, without a last name. The city had a last name, the woman did not.

The noise was unbearable, alternating between the banging-shattering sound and an electronic pulse of varied pitch. He listened to the music and thought of what the radiologist had said, that once it's over, in her Russian accent, you forget instantly the whole experience so how bad can it be, she said, and he thought this sounded like a description of dying. But that was another matter, wasn't it, in another kind of noise, and the trapped man does not come sliding out of his tube. He listened to the music. He tried hard to hear the flutes and distinguish them from the clarinets, if there were clarinets, but he was unable to do this and the only countervailing force was Nancy Dinnerstein drunk in Boston and it gave him a dumb and helpless hard-on, thinking of her in his drafty hotel room with a limited view of the river.

He heard the voice in his headset saying that the next sequence of noise would last seven minutes.

She saw the face in the newspaper, the man from Flight 11. Only one of the nineteen seemed to have a face at this point, staring out of the photo, taut, with hard eyes that seemed too knowing to belong to a face on a driver's license.

She got a call from Carol Shoup, an executive editor with a large publishing house. Carol had occasional jobs for Lianne, who edited books freelance, working usually at home or in the library.

It was Carol who'd sent the postcard from Rome, from the Keats-Shelley House, and she was the sort of person who was sure to sing out, on her return, "Did you get my card?"

Always in a voice that hovered between desperate insecurity and incipient resentment.

Instead she said softly, "Is this a bad time?"

After he walked in the door and people began to hear about it, in the days to come, they called her and said, "Is this a bad time?"

Of course they meant, Are you busy, you must be busy, there must be so much going on, should I call back, can I do something, how is he, will he stay for a while and, finally, can we have dinner, the four of us, somewhere quiet?

It was strange, how terse she became, and uninformative, coming to hate the phrase, marked as it was by nothing more than its own replicating DNA, and to distrust the voices, so smoothly funereal.

"Because if it is," Carol said, "we can talk whenever."

She didn't want to believe she was being selfish in her guardianship of the survivor, determined to hold exclusive rights. This is where he wanted to be, outside the tide of voices and faces, God and country, sitting alone in still rooms, with those nearby who mattered.

"Which, by the way," Carol said, "did you get the card I sent?"

She heard music coming from somewhere in the building, on a lower floor, and took two steps to the door, moving the telephone away from her ear, and then she opened the door and stood there, listening.

———

Now she stood at the foot of the bed and watched him lying there, late one night, after she'd finished working, and asked him finally and quietly.

"Why did you come here?"

"That's the question, isn't it?"

"For Justin, yes?"

This was the answer she wanted because it made the most sense.

"So he could see you were alive," she said.

But it was also only half the answer and she realized she needed to hear something beyond this, a broader motive for his action or intuition or whatever it was.

He thought for a long moment.

"It's hard to reconstruct. I don't know how my mind was working. A guy came along in a van, a plumber, I think, and he drove me here. His radio had been stolen and he knew from the sirens that something was going on but he didn't know what. At some point he had a clear view downtown but all he could see was one tower. He thought one tower was blocking his view of the other tower, or the smoke was. He saw the smoke. He drove east a ways and looked again and there was only one tower. One tower made no sense. Then he turned uptown because that's where he was going and finally he saw me and picked me up. By this time the second tower was gone. Eight radios in three years, he said. All stolen. An electrician, I think. He had a water bottle he kept pushing in my face."

"Your apartment, you knew you couldn't go there."

"I knew the building was too close to the towers and maybe I knew I couldn't go there and maybe I wasn't even thinking about that. Either way, that's not why I came here. It was more than that."

She felt better now.

"He wanted to take me to the hospital, the guy in the van, but I told him to bring me here."

He looked at her.

"I gave him this address," he said for emphasis, and she felt better still.

It was a simple matter, outpatient surgery, a ligament or cartilage, with Lianne in the reception area waiting to take him back to the apartment. On the table he thought of his buddy Rumsey, briefly, just before or after he lost sensation. The doctor, the anesthetist, injected him with a heavy sedative or other agent, a substance containing a memory suppressant, or maybe there were two shots, but there was Rumsey in his chair by the window, which meant the memory was not suppressed or the substance hadn't taken effect yet, a dream, a waking image, whatever it was, Rumsey in the smoke, things coming down.

She stepped into the street thinking ordinary thoughts, dinner, dry cleaning, cash machine, that's it, go home.

There was serious work to do on the book she was editing, for a university press, on ancient alphabets, deadline approaching. There was definitely that.

She wondered what the kid would make of the mango chutney she'd bought, or maybe he'd had it already, had it and hated it, at the Siblings', because Katie talked about it once, or someone did.

The author was a Bulgarian writing in English.

And there was this, the taxis in broad ranks, three or four deep, speeding toward her from the traffic light one block down the avenue as she paused in midcrossing to work out her fate.

In Santa Fe she'd come across a sign on a shop window, for ethnic shampoo. She was traveling in New Mexico with a man she used to see during the separation, a TV executive, flauntingly well-read, teeth lasered lime white, a man who loved her longish face and sort of lazy-lithe body, he said, down to the knobby extremities, and the way he examined her, finger tracing the twists and ridges, which he named after geologic eras, making her laugh, intermittently, for a day and a half, or maybe it was just the altitude at which they were screwing, in the skies of the high desert.

Running toward the far curb now, feeling like a skirt and blouse without a body, how good it felt, hiding behind the plastic shimmer of the dry cleaner's long sheath, which she held at arm's length, between her and the taxis, in self-defense. She imagined the eyes of the drivers, intense and slit, heads pressed toward steering wheels, and there was still the question of her need to be equal to the situation, as Martin had said, her mother's lover.

There was that, and Keith in the shower this morning, standing numbly in the flow, a dim figure far away inside plexiglass.

But what made her think of this, ethnic shampoo, in the middle of Third Avenue, which was a question probably not answerable in a book on ancient alphabets, meticulous decipherments, inscriptions on baked clay, tree bark, stone, bone, sedge. The joke, at her expense, is that the work in question was typed on an old manual machine with textual emendations made by the author in a deeply soulful and unreadable script.

The first cop told him to go to the checkpoint one block east of here and he did this and there were military police and troops in Humvees and a convoy of dump trucks and sanitation sweepers moving south through the parted sawhorse barriers. He showed proof of address with picture ID and the second cop told him to go to the next checkpoint, east of here, and he did this and saw a chain-link barrier stretching down the middle of Broadway, patrolled by troops in gas masks. He told the cop at the checkpoint that he had a cat to feed and if it died his child would be devastated and the man was sympathetic but told him to try the next checkpoint. There were fire-rescue cars and ambulances, there were state police cruisers, flatbed trucks, vehicles with cherry pickers, all moving through the barricades and into the shroud of sand and ash.

He showed the next cop his proof of address and picture ID and told him there were cats he had to feed, three of them, and if they died his children would be devastated and he showed the splint on his left arm. He had to move out of the way when a drove of enormous bulldozers and backhoes moved through the parted barricades, making the sound of hell machines at endless revving pitch. He started over again with the cop and showed his wrist splint and said he needed only fifteen minutes in the apartment to feed the cats and then he'd go back uptown to the hotel, no animals allowed, and reassure the children. The cop said okay but if you're stopped down there be sure to tell them you went through the Broadway checkpoint, not this one.

He worked his way through the frozen zone, south and west, passing through smaller checkpoints and detouring around others. There was a Guard troop in battle jackets and sidearms and now and then he saw a figure in a dust mask, man or woman, obscure and furtive, the only other civilians. The streets and cars were surfaced in ash and there were garbage bags stacked high at curbstones and against the sides of buildings. He walked slowly, watching for something he could not identify. Everything was gray, it was limp and failed, storefronts behind corrugated steel shutters, a city somewhere else, under permanent siege, and a stink in the air that infiltrated the skin.

He stood at the National Rent-A-Fence barrier and looked into the haze, seeing the strands of bent filigree that were the last standing things, a skeletal remnant of the tower where he'd worked for ten years. The dead were everywhere, in the air, in the rubble, on rooftops nearby, in the breezes that carried from the river. They were settled in ash and drizzled on windows all along the streets, in his hair and on his clothes.

He realized someone had joined him at the fence, a man in a dust mask who maintained a calculated silence designed to be broken.

"Look at it," he said finally. "I say to myself I'm standing here. It's hard to believe, being here and seeing it."

His words were muffled by the mask.

"I walked to Brooklyn when it happened," he said. "I don't live there. I live way uptown on the west side but I work down around here and when it happened everybody was walking across the bridge to Brooklyn and I went with them. I walked across the bridge because they were walking across the bridge."

It sounded like a speech defect, the words smothered and blurred. He took out his cell phone and entered a number.

"I'm standing here," he said but had to repeat himself because the person he was talking to could not hear him clearly.

"I'm standing here," he said.

Keith headed in the direction of his apartment building. He saw three men in hard hats and NYPD windbreakers, with search dogs on short leads. They came walking toward him and one of the men tilted his head in inquiry. Keith told him where he was going, mentioned the cats and the children. The man paused to tell him that the tower at One Liberty Plaza, fifty-plus stories, near where Keith was going, was about to fucking fall down. The other men stood by impatiently and the first man told him that the building was actually and measurably moving. He nodded and waited for them to leave and went south once more and then west again through mostly empty streets. Two Hasidic men stood outside a shop with a broken window. They looked a thousand years old. When he approached his building he saw workers in respirators and protective body suits scouring the sidewalk with a massive vacuum pump.

The front doors were blown in or kicked in. It was not looters, he thought. He thought that people had taken desperate shelter, taken cover wherever they could when the towers came down. The entrance hall reeked of garbage uncollected in the basement. He knew that the electricity had been restored and there was no reason not to take the elevator but he climbed the nine flights to his apartment, pausing on floors three and seven to stand at the near end of the long corridors. He stood and listened. The building seemed empty, it felt and sounded empty. When he entered his apartment he stood a while, just looking around. The windows were scabbed in sand and ash and there were fragments of paper and one whole sheet trapped in the grime. Everything else was the same as it had been when he walked out the door for work that Tuesday morning. Not that he'd noticed. He'd lived here for a year and a half, since the separation, finding a place close to the office, centering his life, content with the narrowest of purviews, that of not noticing.

But now he looked. Some light entered between splashes of window grit. He saw the place differently now. Here he was, seen clear, with nothing that mattered to him in these two and a half rooms, dim and still, in a faint odor of nonoccupancy. There was the card table, that was all, with its napped green surface, baize or felt, site of the weekly poker game. One of the players said baize, which is imitation felt, he said, and Keith more or less conceded this. It was the one uncomplicated interval of his week, his month, the poker game—the one anticipation that was not marked by the bloodguilt tracings of severed connections. Call or fold. Felt or baize.

This was the last time he would stand here. There were no cats, there were only clothes. He put some things in a suitcase, a few shirts and trousers and his trekking boots from Switzerland and to hell with the rest. This and that and the Swiss boots because the boots mattered and the poker table mattered but he wouldn't need the table, two players dead, one badly injured. A single suitcase, that was all, and his passport, checkbooks, birth certificate and a few other documents, the state papers of identity. He stood and looked and felt something so lonely he could touch it with his hand. At the window the intact page stirred in the breeze and he went over to see if it was readable. Instead he looked at the visible sliver of One Liberty Plaza and began to count the floors, losing interest about halfway up, thinking of something else.

He looked in the refrigerator. Maybe he was thinking of the man who used to live here and he checked the bottles and cartons for a clue. The paper rustled at the window and he picked up the suitcase and walked out the door, locking it behind him. He went about fifteen paces into the corridor, away from the stairwell, and spoke in a voice slightly above a whisper.

He said, "I'm standing here," and then, louder, "I'm standing here."

In the movie version, someone would be in the building, an emotionally damaged woman or a homeless old man, and there would be dialogue and close-ups.

The truth is that he was wary of the elevator. He didn't want to know this but did, unavoidably. He walked down to the lobby, smelling the garbage coming closer with every step he took. The men with the vacuum pump were gone. He heard the drone and grind of heavy machinery at the site, earthmoving equipment, excavators that pounded concrete to dust, and then the sound of a klaxon that signaled danger, possible collapse of a structure nearby. He waited, they all waited, and then the grind began again.

He went to the local post office to pick up his undelivered mail and then walked north toward the barricades, thinking it might be hard to find a taxi at a time when every cabdriver in New York was named Muhammad.

4

Their separation had been marked by a certain symmetry, the steadfast commitment each made to an equivalent group. He had his poker game, six players, downtown, one night a week. She had her storyline sessions, in East Harlem, also weekly, in the afternoon, a gathering of five or six or seven men and women in the early stages of Alzheimer's disease.

The card games ended after the towers fell but the sessions took on a measure of intensity. The members sat on folding chairs in a room with a makeshift plywood door in a large community center. A steady bang and clatter bounced off the hallway walls. There were children racing around, adults in special classes. There were people playing dominoes and ping-pong, volunteers preparing food deliveries to elderly people in the area.

The group had been started by a clinical psychologist who left Lianne alone to conduct these meetings, which were strictly for morale. She and the members talked a while about events in the world and in their lives and then she handed out lined pads and ballpoint pens and suggested a topic they might write about or asked them to choose one. Remembering my father, that sort of thing, or What I always wanted to do but never did, or Do my children know who I am.

They wrote for roughly twenty minutes and then each, in turn, read aloud what he or she had written. Sometimes it scared her, the first signs of halting response, the losses and failings, the grim prefigurings that issued now and then from a mind beginning to slide away from the adhesive friction that makes an individual possible. It was in the language, the inverted letters, the lost word at the end of a struggling sentence. It was in the handwriting that might melt into runoff. But there were a thousand high times the members experienced, given a chance to encounter the crossing points of insight and memory that the act of writing allows. They laughed loud and often. They worked into themselves, finding narratives that rolled and tumbled, and how natural it seemed to do this, tell stories about themselves.

Rosellen S. saw her father walk in the door after a disappearance lasting four years. He was bearded now, head shaved, one arm missing. She was ten when this happened and she described the event in a run-on convergence, an intimacy of clean physical detail and dreamy reminiscence that had no seeming connection—radio programs, cousins named Luther, two of them, and a dress her mother wore to somebody's wedding, and they listened to her read in a half whisper, *one arm missing*, and Benny in the next chair closed his eyes and rocked all through the telling. This was their prayer room, said Omar H. They summoned the force of final authority. No one knew what they knew, here in the last clear minute before it all closed down.

They signed their pages with first name and first letter of last name. This was Lianne's idea, maybe a little affected, she thought, as if they were characters in European novels. They were characters and authors both, able to tell what they wished, cradle the rest in silence. When Carmen G. read her pieces she liked to embellish them with phrases in Spanish to seize the auditory core of an incident or an emotion. Benny T. hated to

write, loved to talk. He brought pastry to the meetings, large jel-
lied bladders that no one else would touch. The noise echoed in
the hallway, kids playing piano and drums, others on roller
skates, and the voices and accents of the adults, their polyglot
English floating through the building.

Members wrote about hard times, happy memories, daugh-
ters becoming mothers. Anna wrote about the revelation of
writing itself, how she hadn't known she could write ten words
and now look what comes pouring out. This was Anna C., a
broad-bodied woman from the neighborhood. Nearly all of them
were from the neighborhood, the eldest being Curtis B., eighty-
one, a tall taciturn man with a prison history and a voice, in his
readings, that had the resonance of entries in the *Encyclopaedia
Britannica*, a collection he'd read front to back in the peniten-
tiary library.

There was one subject the members wanted to write about,
insistently, all of them but Omar H. It made Omar nervous but
he agreed in the end. They wanted to write about the planes.

When he got back uptown the apartment was empty. He sorted
through his mail. His name was misspelled on a couple of pieces
of mail, this was not unusual, and he snatched a ballpoint pen
from the mug near the telephone and made the corrections on
the envelopes. He wasn't sure when he'd started doing this and
didn't know why he did it. There was no reason why. Because it
wasn't him, with the name misspelled, that's why. He did it and
then kept doing it and maybe he understood at some snake-brain
level of perception that he had to do it and would keep doing it
down the years and into the decades. He did not construct this
future in clear terms but it was probably there, humming under
the skull. He never corrected the spelling on mail that was out-

31

right third-class indiscriminate throwaway advertising matter. He almost did, the first time, but then did not. Junk mail was created for just this reason, to presort the world's identities into one, with his or her name misspelled. In most other cases he made the correction, involving one letter in the first syllable of his last name, which was Neudecker, and then slit open the envelope. He never made the correction in the presence of someone else. It was an act he was careful to conceal.

She walked across Washington Square Park behind a student saying *hopefully* into his cell phone. It was a bright day, chess players at their tables, a fashion shoot in progress under the arch. They said *hopefully*. They said *oh my god*, in delight and small awe. She saw a young woman reading on a bench, in the lotus position. Lianne used to read haiku, sitting crosslegged on the floor, in the weeks and months after her father died. She thought of a poem by Bashō, or the first and third lines. She didn't remember the second line. *Even in Kyoto—I long for Kyoto.* The second line was missing but she didn't think she needed it.

Half an hour later she was in Grand Central Station to meet her mother's train. She hadn't been here lately and was not accustomed to the sight of police and state troopers in tight clusters or guardsmen with dogs. Other places, she thought, other worlds, dusty terminals, major intersections, this is routine and always will be. This was not a considered reflection so much as a flutter, a downdraft of memory, cities she'd seen, crowds and heat. But the normal order was also in evidence here, tourists taking pictures, commuters in running flurries. She was headed to the information desk to check the gate number when something caught her eyes out near the approach to 42nd Street.

There were people clustered near the entrance, on both

sides, others pushing through the doors but seemingly still engaged by something happening outside. She made her way out onto the crowded sidewalk. Traffic was building, a few horns blowing. She edged along a storefront and looked up toward the green steel structure that passes over Pershing Square, the section of elevated roadway that carries traffic around the terminal in both directions.

A man was dangling there, above the street, upside down. He wore a business suit, one leg bent up, arms at his sides. A safety harness was barely visible, emerging from his trousers at the straightened leg and fastened to the decorative rail of the viaduct.

She'd heard of him, a performance artist known as Falling Man. He'd appeared several times in the last week, unannounced, in various parts of the city, suspended from one or another structure, always upside down, wearing a suit, a tie and dress shoes. He brought it back, of course, those stark moments in the burning towers when people fell or were forced to jump. He'd been seen dangling from a balcony in a hotel atrium and police had escorted him out of a concert hall and two or three apartment buildings with terraces or accessible rooftops.

Traffic was barely moving now. There were people shouting up at him, outraged at the spectacle, the puppetry of human desperation, a body's last fleet breath and what it held. It held the gaze of the world, she thought. There was the awful openness of it, something we'd not seen, the single falling figure that trails a collective dread, body come down among us all. And now, she thought, this little theater piece, disturbing enough to stop traffic and send her back into the terminal.

Her mother was waiting at the gate, on the lower level, leaning on her cane.

She said, "I had to get out of there."

"I thought you'd stay another week at least. Better there than here."

"I want to be in my apartment."

"What about Martin?"

"Martin is still there. We're still arguing. I want to sit in my armchair and read my Europeans."

Lianne took the bag and they rode the escalator up to the main concourse, steeped in dusty light slanting through the high lunettes. A dozen people were grouped around a guide near the staircase to the east balcony, gazing at the sky ceiling, the gold-leaf constellations, with a guardsman and his dog standing alongside, and her mother could not help commenting on the man's uniform, the question of jungle camouflage in midtown Manhattan.

"People are leaving, you're coming back."

"Nobody's leaving," her mother said. "The ones who leave were never here."

"I have to admit, I've thought of it. Take the kid and go."

"Don't make me sick," her mother said.

Even in New York, she thought. Of course she was wrong about the second line of the haiku. She knew this. Whatever the line was, it was surely crucial to the poem. *Even in New York—I long for New York.*

She led her mother across the concourse and along a passage that would bring them out three blocks north of the main entrance. There would be moving traffic there and cabs to hail and no sign of the man who was upside down, in stationary fall, ten days after the planes.

It's interesting, isn't it? To sleep with your husband, a thirty-eight-year-old woman and a thirty-nine-year-old man, and never a breathy sound of sex. He's your ex-husband who was never technically ex, the stranger you married in another lifetime. She dressed and undressed, he watched and did not. It was strange but interesting. A tension did not build. This was extremely strange. She wanted him here, nearby, but felt no edge of self-contradiction or self-denial. Just waiting, that was all, a broad pause in recognition of a thousand sour days and nights, not so easily set aside. The matter needed time. It could not happen the way things did in normal course. And it's interesting, isn't it, the way you move about the bedroom, routinely near-naked, and the respect you show the past, the deference to its fervors of the wrong kind, its passions of cut and burn.

She wanted contact and so did he.

The briefcase was smaller than normal and reddish brown with brass hardware, sitting on the closet floor. He'd seen it there before but understood for the first time that it wasn't his. Wasn't his wife's, wasn't his. He'd seen it, even half placed it in some long-lost distance as an object in his hand, the right hand, an object pale with ash, but it wasn't until now that he knew why it was here.

He picked it up and took it to the desk in the study. It was here because he'd brought it here. It wasn't his briefcase but he'd carried it out of the tower and he had it with him when he showed up at the door. She'd cleaned it since then, obviously, and he stood and looked at it, full-grain leather with a pebbled texture, nicely burnished over time, one of the front buckles bearing a singe mark. He ran his thumb over the padded handle, trying to remember why he'd carried it out of there. He was in no hurry to open it. He began to think he didn't want to open it but wasn't sure why. He ran his knuckles over the front flap and unbuckled one of the straps. Sunlight fell across the star map on the wall. He unbuckled the second strap.

He found a set of headphones and a CD player. There was a small bottle of spring water. There was a cell phone in the pocket designed for that purpose and half a chocolate bar in a slot for business cards. He noted three pen sleeves, one rollerball pen. There was a pack of Kent cigarettes and a lighter. In one of the saddle pockets he found a sonic toothbrush in a travel case and a digital voice recorder as well, sleeker than his own.

He examined the items with detachment. It was somehow morbidly unright to be doing this but he was so remote from the things in the briefcase, from the occasion of the briefcase, that it probably didn't matter.

There was an imitation leather folio with a blank notebook in one of the pockets. He found a stamped envelope preaddressed to AT&T, no return address, and a book in the zippered compartment, paperback, a guide to buying used cars. The CD in the player was a compilation of music from Brazil.

The wallet with money, credit cards and a driver's license was in the other saddle pocket.

This time the woman showed up in the bakery, mother of the Siblings. She walked in just after Lianne did and joined her in line after taking a number from the dispenser on the counter.

"I'm just wondering about the binoculars. He's not, you know, the most outgoing child."

She smiled at Lianne, warmly and falsely, in a fragrance of glazed cakes, a mother-to-mother look, like we both know how these kids have enormous gleaming worlds they don't share with their parents.

"Because he always has them lately. I just wondered, you know, what he might have told you one way or the other."

Lianne didn't know what she was talking about. She looked into the broad and florid face of the man behind the counter. The answer wasn't there.

"He shares them with my kids, so that's not it, because their father promised them a pair but we haven't gotten around, you know, binoculars, not the highest priority, and my Katie's being supersecret and her brother's her brother, loyal to a fault."

"You mean what are they looking at, behind closed doors?"

"I thought maybe Justin."

"Can't be much, can it? Maybe hawks. You know about the red-tails."

"No, it's definitely something to do with Bill Lawton. I'm sure of this, absolutely, because the binoculars are part of the whole hush-hush syndrome these kids are engulfed in."

"Bill Lawton."

"The man. The name I mentioned."

"I don't think so," Lianne said.

"This is their secret. I know the name but that's all. And I thought maybe Justin. Because my kids totally blank out when I bring up the subject."

She didn't know that Justin was taking the binoculars on his visits to the Siblings. They weren't his binoculars exactly, although she guessed it was all right for him to use them without permission. But maybe not, she thought, waiting for the man to call her number.

"Aren't they doing birds in school?"

"Last time it was clouds."

"Turns out I was wrong about the clouds. But they're definitely studying birds and birdcalls and habitats," she told the woman. "They go trekking through Central Park."

She realized how much she hated to stand in line with a number in her fist. She hated this regimen of assigned numbers, strictly enforced, in a confined space, with nothing at the end of the process but a small white bow-tied box of pastry.

He wasn't sure what it was that woke him up. He lay there, eyes open, thinking into the dark. Then he began to hear it, out on the stairs and along the hall, coming from a lower floor somewhere, music, and he listened carefully now, hand drums and stringed instruments and massed voices in the walls, but soft, but seemingly far off, on the other side of a valley, it seemed, men in chanted prayer, voices in chorus in praise of God.

Allah-uu   *Allah-uu*   *Allah-uu*

There was an old-fashioned pencil sharpener clamped to the end of the table in Justin's room. She stood at the door and watched him insert each pencil in the slot and then crank the handle. He had red-and-blue combination pencils, Cedar Pointe pencils, Dixon Trimlines, vintage Eberhard Fabers. He had pencils from hotels in Zurich and Hong Kong. There were pencils fashioned from tree bark, rough and knotted. There were pencils from the design store of the Museum of Modern Art. He had Mirado Black Warriors. He had pencils from a SoHo shop that were inscribed along the shaft with cryptic sayings from Tibet.

It was awful in a way, all these fragments of status washing up in some little kid's room.

But what she loved to watch was the way he blew the microscopic shavings off the pencil point after he finished sharpening. If he were to do it all day, she'd watch all day, pencil after pencil.

He'd crank and blow, crank and blow, a ritual more thorough and righteous than the formal signing of some document of state by eleven men with medals.

When he saw her watching he said, "What?"

"I talked to Katie's mother today. Katie and what's-his-name. She told me about the binoculars."

He stood and watched her, pencil in hand.

"Katie and what's-his-name."

"Robert," he said.

"Her little brother Robert. And his older sister Katie. And this man the three of you keep talking about. Is this something I should know about?"

"What man?" he said.

"What man. And what binoculars," she said. "Are you supposed to take the binoculars out of the house without permission?"

He stood and watched. He had pale hair, his father's, and a certain somberness of body, a restraint, his own, that gave him an uncanny discipline in games, in physical play.

"Did your father give you permission?"

He stood and watched.

"What's so interesting about the view from that room? You can tell me that, can't you?"

She leaned against the door, prepared to remain for three, four, five days, in the context of parental body language, or until he answered.

He moved one hand away from his body, slightly, the hand without the pencil, palm up, and executed the faintest change in facial expression, causing an arched indentation between the chin and lower lip, like an old man's mute version of the young boy's opening remark, which was "What?"

———

He sat alongside the table, left forearm placed along the near edge, hand dangling from the adjoining edge, curled into a gentle fist. He raised the hand without lifting his forearm and kept it in the air for five seconds. He did this ten times.

It was their term, *gentle fist*, the rehab center's term, used in the instruction sheet.

He found these sessions restorative, four times a day, the wrist extensions, the ulnar deviations. These were the true countermeasures to the damage he'd suffered in the tower, in the descending chaos. It was not the MRI and not the surgery that brought him closer to well-being. It was this modest home program, the counting of seconds, the counting of repetitions, the times of day he reserved for the exercises, the ice he applied following each set of exercises.

There were the dead and maimed. His injury was slight but it wasn't the torn cartilage that was the subject of this effort. It was the chaos, the levitation of ceilings and floors, the voices choking in smoke. He sat in deep concentration, working on the hand shapes, the bend of the wrist toward the floor, the bend of the wrist toward the ceiling, the forearm flat on the table, the thumb-up configuration in certain setups, the use of the uninvolved hand to apply pressure to the involved hand. He washed his splint in warm soapy water. He did not adjust his splint without consulting the therapist. He read the instruction sheet. He curled the hand into a gentle fist.

Jack Glenn, her father, did not want to submit to the long course of senile dementia. He made a couple of phone calls from his cabin in northern New Hampshire and then used an old sporting rifle to kill himself. She did not know the details. She was twenty-two when this happened and did not ask the local police for details. What detail might there be that was not unbearable? But she had to wonder if it was the rifle she knew, the one he'd let her grip and aim, but not fire, the time she'd joined him in the woods, as a fourteen-year-old, in a halfhearted hunt for varmints. She was a city girl and not completely sure what a varmint was but clearly recalled something he'd said to her that day. He liked to talk about the anatomy of racecars, motorcycles, hunting rifles, how things work, and she liked to listen. It was a mark of the distance between them that she listened so eagerly, the perennial miles, the weeks and months.

He'd hefted the weapon and said to her, "The shorter the barrel, the stronger the muzzle blast."

The force of that term, *muzzle blast*, carried through the years. The news of his death seemed to ride on the arc of those two words. They were awful words but she tried to tell herself he'd done a brave thing. It was way too soon. There was time before the disease took solid hold but Jack was always respectful of nature's little fuckups and figured the deal was sealed. She wanted to believe that the rifle that killed him was the one he'd braced against her shoulder among the stands of tamarack and spruce in the plunging light of that northern day.

Martin embraced her in the doorway, gravely. He'd been some-where in Europe when the attacks occurred and was on one of the first transatlantic flights as schedules resumed, erratically.

"Nothing seems exaggerated anymore. Nothing amazes me," he said.

Her mother was in the bedroom dressing for the day, finally, at noon, and Martin walked around the room looking at things, stepping among Justin's toys, noting changes in the placement of objects.

"Somewhere in Europe. This is how I think of you."

"Except when I'm here," he said.

The standing hand, a small bronze normally on the bamboo end table, was now on the wrought-iron table, laden with books, near the window, and the Nevelson wall piece had been replaced by the photograph of Rimbaud.

"But even when you're here, I think of you coming from a distant city on your way to another distant city and neither place has shape or form."

"This is me, I am shapeless," he said.

They talked about events. They talked about the things everyone was talking about. He followed her to the kitchen, where she poured him a beer. She poured and talked.

"People read poems. People I know, they read poetry to ease the shock and pain, give them a kind of space, something beautiful in language," she said, "to bring comfort or composure. I don't read poems. I read newspapers. I put my head in the pages and get angry and crazy."

"There's another approach, which is to study the matter. Stand apart and think about the elements," he said. "Coldly, clearly if you're able to. Do not let it tear you down. See it, measure it."

"Measure it," she said.

"There's the event, there's the individual. Measure it. Let it teach you something. See it. Make yourself equal to it."

Martin Ridnour was an art dealer, a collector, an investor perhaps. She wasn't sure what he did exactly or how he did it but suspected that he bought art and then flipped it, quickly, for large profit. She liked him. He spoke with an accent and had an apartment here and an office in Basel. He spent time in Berlin. He did or did not have a wife in Paris.

They were back in the living room, he with the glass in one hand, bottle in the other.

"Probably I don't know what I'm talking about," he said. "You talk, I will drink."

Martin was overweight but did not appear ripe with good living. He was usually jet-lagged, more or less unwashed, in a well-worn suit, trying to resemble an old poet in exile, her mother said. He was not quite bald, with a shadow of gray bristle on his head and a beard that looked about two weeks old, mostly gray and never groomed.

"I called Nina when I got in this morning. We're going away for a week or two."

"Good idea."

"Handsome old house in Connecticut, by the shore."

"You arrange things."

"This is something I do, yes."

"I have a question, unrelated. You can ignore it," she said. "A question from nowhere."

She looked at him, standing behind the armchair across the room, draining his glass.

"Do the two of you have sex? It's none of my business. But can you have sex? I mean considering the knee replacement. She's not doing the exercises."

He took the bottle and glass toward the kitchen, responding over his shoulder with some amusement.

"She doesn't have sex with her knee. We bypass the knee. The knee is damn tender. But we work around it."

She waited for him to return.

"None of my business. But she seems to be entering a kind of withdrawal. And I just wondered."

"And you," he said. "And Keith. He's back with you now. This is true?"

"Could leave tomorrow. Nobody knows."

"But he's staying in your flat."

"It's early. I don't know what will happen. We sleep together, yes, if that's what you're asking. But only technically."

He showed quizzical interest.

"Share a bed. Innocently," he said.

"Yes."

"I like this. How many nights?"

"He spent the first night in the hospital for observation. Since then, whatever it is. This is Monday. Six days, five nights."

"I will be asking for progress reports," he said.

He'd talked to Keith a couple of times only. This was an American, not a New Yorker, not one of the Manhattan elect, a group maintained by controlled propagation. He tried to gain a sense of the younger man's feelings about politics and religion, the voice and manner of the heartland. All he learned was that Keith had once owned a pit bull. This, at least, seemed to mean something, a dog that was all skull and jaws, an American breed, developed originally to fight and kill.

"One of these days maybe you and Keith will have a chance to talk again."

"About women, I think."

"Mother and daughter. All the sordid details," she said.

"I like Keith. I told him a story once that he enjoyed. About cardplayers. He's a cardplayer of course. About cardplayers I used to know and about the seating arrangement they maintained at their weekly game, for nearly half a century. Longer actually. He enjoyed this story."

Her mother came in, Nina, in a dark skirt and white blouse, leaning on her cane. Martin held her briefly and then watched her settle into the chair, slowly, in segmental movements.

"What old dead wars we fight. I think in these past days we've lost a thousand years," she said.

Martin had been away for a month. He was seeing the last

stage of the transformation, her embrace of age, the studied attitude that weaves easily through the fact itself. Lianne felt a sadness on his behalf. Has her mother's hair gone whiter? Is she taking too much pain medication? Did she have a minor stroke at that conference in Chicago? And, finally, was he lying about their sexual activity? Her mind is fine. She is not so forgiving of the normal erosions, the names she now and then forgets, the location of an object she has just, seconds ago, put somewhere. But she is alert to what is important, the broad surround, to other states of being.

"Tell us what they're doing in Europe."

"They're being kind to Americans," he said.

"Tell us what you've bought and sold."

"What I can tell you is that the art market will stagnate. Activity here and there in modern masters. Otherwise dismal prospects."

"Modern masters. I'm relieved," Nina said.

"Trophy art."

"People need their trophies."

He seemed heartened by her sarcasm.

"I've just barely set foot in the door. In the country in fact. What does she do? She gives me grief."

"This is her job," Lianne said.

They'd known each other for twenty years, Martin and Nina, lovers for much of that time, New York, Berkeley, somewhere in Europe. Lianne knew that the defensive stance he took at times was an aspect of their private manner of address, not the stain of something deeper. He was not the shapeless man he claimed to be or physically mimicked. He was unflinching in fact, and smart in his work, and gracious to her, and generous to her mother. The two beautiful Morandi still lifes were gifts from Martin. The passport photos on the opposite wall, Martin also, from his collection, aged documents, stamped and faded, history measured in inches, and also beautiful.

Lianne said, "Who wants to eat?"

Nina wanted to smoke. The bamboo end table stood next to the armchair now and held an ashtray, a lighter and a pack of cigarettes.

Her mother lit up. She watched, Lianne did, feeling something familiar and a little painful, how Nina at a certain point began to consider her invisible. The memory was located there, in the way she snapped shut the lighter and put it down, in the hand gesture and the drifting smoke.

"Dead wars, holy wars. God could appear in the sky tomorrow."

"Whose God would it be?" Martin said.

"God used to be an urban Jew. He's back in the desert now."

Lianne's studies were meant to take her into deeper scholarship, into serious work in languages or art history. She'd traveled through Europe and much of the Middle East but it was tourism in the end, with shallow friends, not determined inquiry into beliefs, institutions, languages, art, or so said Nina Bartos.

"It's sheer panic. They attack out of panic."

"This much, yes, it may be true. Because they think the world is a disease. This world, this society, ours. A disease that's spreading," he said.

"There are no goals they can hope to achieve. They're not liberating a people or casting out a dictator. Kill the innocent, only that."

"They strike a blow to this country's dominance. They achieve this, to show how a great power can be vulnerable. A power that interferes, that occupies."

He spoke softly, looking into the carpet.

"One side has the capital, the labor, the technology, the

armies, the agencies, the cities, the laws, the police and the prisons. The other side has a few men willing to die."

"God is great," she said.

"Forget God. These are matters of history. This is politics and economics. All the things that shape lives, millions of people, dispossessed, their lives, their consciousness."

"It's not the history of Western interference that pulls down these societies. It's their own history, their mentality. They live in a closed world, of choice, of necessity. They haven't advanced because they haven't wanted to or tried to."

"They use the language of religion, okay, but this is not what drives them."

"Panic, this is what drives them."

Her mother's anger submerged her own. She deferred to it. She saw the hard tight fury in Nina's face and felt, herself, only a sadness, hearing these two people, joined in spirit, take strongly opposing positions.

Then Martin eased off, voice going soft again.

"All right, yes, it may be true."

"Blame us. Blame us for their failures."

"All right, yes. But this is not an attack on one country, one or two cities. All of us, we are targets now."

They were still talking ten minutes later when Lianne left the room. She stood in the bathroom looking in the mirror. The moment seemed false to her, a scene in a movie when a character tries to understand what is going on in her life by looking in the mirror.

She was thinking, Keith is alive.

Keith had been alive for six days now, ever since he appeared at the door, and what would this mean to her, what would this do to her and to her son?

She washed her hands and face. Then she went to the cabinet and got a fresh towel and dried herself. After she tossed the towel in the hamper she flushed the toilet. She didn't flush the toilet to make the others think she'd left the living room for a compelling reason. The flushing toilet wasn't audible in the living room. This was for her own pointless benefit, flushing. Maybe it was meant to mark the end of the interval, to get her out of here.

What was she doing here? She was being a child, she thought.

The talk had begun to fade by the time she returned. He had more to say, Martin, but possibly thought this was not the moment, not now, too soon, and he wandered over to the Morandi paintings on the wall.

It was only seconds later that Nina dropped into a light sleep. She was taking a round of medications, a mystical wheel, the ritualistic design of the hours and days in tablets and capsules, in colors, shapes and numbers. Lianne watched her. It was difficult to see her fitted so steadfastly to a piece of furniture, resigned and unstirring, the energetic arbiter of her daughter's life, ever discerning, the woman who'd given birth to the word *beautiful*, for what excites admiration in art, ideas, objects, in the faces of men and women, the mind of a child. All this dwindling to a human breath.

Her mother wasn't dying, was she? Lighten up, she thought.

She opened her eyes, finally, and the two women looked at each other. It was a sustained moment and Lianne did not know, could not have put into words what it was they were sharing. Or she knew but could not name the overlapping emotions. It was what there was between them, meaning every minute together and apart, what they'd known and felt and what would come next, in the minutes, days and years.

Martin stood before the paintings.

"I'm looking at these objects, kitchen objects but removed from the kitchen, free of the kitchen, the house, everything practical and functioning. And I must be back in another time zone. I must be even more disoriented than usual after a long flight," he said, pausing. "Because I keep seeing the towers in this still life."

Lianne joined him at the wall. The painting in question showed seven or eight objects, the taller ones set against a brushy slate background. The other items were huddled boxes and biscuit tins, grouped before a darker background. The full array, in unfixed perspective and mostly muted colors, carried an odd spare power.

They looked together.

Two of the taller items were dark and somber, with smoky marks and smudges, and one of them was partly concealed by a long-necked bottle. The bottle was a bottle, white. The two dark objects, too obscure to name, were the things that Martin was referring to.

"What do you see?" he said.

She saw what he saw. She saw the towers.

5

He entered the park at the Engineers' Gate, where runners stretched and bent before going out on the track. The day was warm and still and he walked along the road that ran parallel to the bridle path. There was somewhere to go but he was in no hurry to get there. He watched an elderly woman on a bench who was thinking distantly of something, holding a pale green apple pressed to her cheek. The road was closed to traffic and he thought you come to the park to see people, the ones who are shadows in the street. There were runners up to the left, on the track around the reservoir, and others on the bridle path just above him and still more runners on the roadway, men with handweights, running, and women running behind baby strollers, pushing babies, and runners with dogs on leashes. You come to the park to see dogs, he thought.

The road bent west and three girls wearing headsets went rollerblading past. The ordinariness, so normally unnoticeable, fell upon him oddly, with almost dreamlike effect. He was carrying the briefcase and wanted to turn back. He crossed up the slope and walked past the tennis courts. There were three horses hitched to the fence, police helmets clipped to their saddlebags. A woman ran past, talking to someone, miserably, on her cell phone, and he wanted to toss the briefcase in the reservoir and go back home.

She lived in a building just off Amsterdam Avenue and he climbed the six flights to her apartment. She seemed tentative, letting him in, even, strangely, a little wary, and he started to explain, as he had on the telephone the day before, that he hadn't meant to delay returning the briefcase. She was saying something about the credit cards in the wallet, that she hadn't canceled them because, well, everything was gone, she thought everything was buried, it was lost and gone, and they stopped talking and then started again, simultaneously, until she made a small gesture of futility. He left the briefcase on a chair by the door and went over to the sofa, saying he could not stay very long.

She was a light-skinned black woman, his age or close, and gentle-seeming, and on the heavy side.

He said, "When I found your name in the briefcase, after I found your name and checked the phone directory and saw you were listed and I'm actually dialing the number, that's when it occurred to me."

"I know what you're going to say."

"I thought why am I doing this without checking further because is this person even alive?"

There was a pause and he realized how softly she'd spoken inside his jumpy commentary.

"I have some herbal tea," she said. "Sparkling water if you like."

"Sparkling water. Spring water. There's a small bottle in the briefcase. Let me think. Poland Spring."

"Poland Spring," she said.

"Anyway if you'd like to check what's in there."

"Of course not. No," she said quietly.

She stood in the entranceway to the kitchen. The small boom of traffic sounded outside the windows.

He said, "See, what happened is I didn't know I had it. It wasn't even a case of forgetting. I don't think I knew."

"I don't think I know your name."

He said, "Keith?"

"Did you tell me this?"

"I think so, yes."

"The phone call was so out of the blue."

"It's Keith," he said.

"Did you work for Preston Webb?"

"No, one floor up. Small outfit called Royer Properties."

He was on his feet now, ready to leave.

"Preston's so sprawling. I thought maybe we just hadn't run into each other."

"No, Royer. We're just about decimated," he said.

"We're waiting to see what happens, where we relocate. I don't think about it much."

There was a silence.

He said, "We were Royer and Stans. Then Stans got indicted."

Finally he moved toward the door and then picked up the briefcase. He paused, reaching for the doorknob, and looked at her, across the room, and she was smiling.

"Why did I do that?"

"Habit," she said.

"I was ready to walk out the door with your property. All over again. Your priceless family heritage. Your cell phone."

"That thing. I stopped needing it when I didn't have it."

"Your toothbrush," he said. "Your pack of cigarettes."

"God, no, my guilty secret. But I'm down to four a day."

She waved him back to the sofa with a broad arc of the arm, a traffic cop's sweeping command to get things going.

She served tea and a plate of sugar cookies. Her name was Florence Givens. She placed a kitchen chair on the other side of the coffee table and sat at a diagonal.

He said, "I know everything about you. A sonic toothbrush. You brush your teeth with sound waves."

"I'm gadget crazy. I love those things."

"Why do you have a better voice recorder than I had?"

"I think I've used it twice."

"I used mine but then never listened. I liked to talk into it."

"What did you say when you talked into it?"

"I don't know. My fellow Americans," he said.

"I thought everything was lost and gone. I didn't report a lost driver's license. I didn't do anything, basically, but sit in this room."

An hour later they were still talking. The cookies were small and awful but he kept nipping into them, unthinkingly, eating only the first baby bite and leaving the mutilated remains to litter the plate.

"I was at my screen and heard the plane approach but only after I was thrown down. That's how fast," she said.

"Are you sure you heard the plane?"

"The impact sent me to the floor and then I heard the plane. I think the sprinklers, I'm trying to recall the sprinklers. I know I was wet at some point, all through."

He understood that she hadn't meant to say this. It sounded intimate, to be wet all through, and she had to pause a moment.

He waited.

"My phone was ringing. I was at my desk now, I don't know, just to sit, to steady myself, and I pick up the phone. Then we're talking, like hello, it's Donna. It's my friend Donna. I

said, Did you hear that? She's calling from home, in Philadel-
phia, to talk about a visit. I said, Did you hear that?"

She went through it slowly, remembering as she spoke, often
pausing to look into space, to see things again, the collapsed ceilings and blocked stairwells, the smoke, always, and the fallen
wall, the drywall, and she paused to search for the word and he
waited, watching.

She was dazed and had no sense of time, she said.

There was water somewhere running or falling, flowing down
from somewhere.

Men ripped their shirts and wound them around their faces,
for masks, for the smoke.

She saw a woman with burnt hair, hair burnt and smoking,
but now she wasn't sure she'd seen this or heard someone say it.

Times they had to walk blind, smoke so thick, hand on the
shoulder of the person in front.

She'd lost her shoes or kicked them off and there was water
like a stream somewhere, nearby, running down a mountain.

The stairwell was crowded now, and slow, with people coming from other floors.

"Someone said, Asthma. Now that I'm talking, it's coming
back a little bit. Asthma, asthma. A woman like desperate. There
were panic faces. That's when I think I fell, I just went down. I
went down five or six steps and hit the landing, like stumble-
falling, and I hit hard."

She wanted to tell him everything. This was clear to him.
Maybe she'd forgotten he was there, in the tower, or maybe he
was the one she needed to tell for precisely that reason. He
knew she hadn't talked about this, not so intensely, to anyone
else.

"It was the panic of being trampled even though they were
careful, they helped me, but it was the feeling of being down in

a crowd and you will be trampled, but they helped me and this one man I remember, helping me get to my feet, elderly man, out of breath, helping me, talking to me until I was able to get going again."

There were flames in elevator shafts.

There was a man talking about a giant earthquake. She forgot all about the plane and was ready to believe an earthquake even though she'd heard a plane. And someone else said, I been in earthquakes, a man in a suit and tie, this ain't no earthquake, a distinguished man, an educated man, an executive, this ain't no earthquake.

There were dangling wires and she felt a wire touch her arm. It touched the man behind her and he jumped and cursed and then laughed.

The crowd on the stairs, the sheer force of it, hobbling, crying, burnt, some of them, but mostly calm, a woman in a wheelchair and they carried her and people made room, bending into single file on the stairs.

Her face held an earnest appeal, a plea of some sort.

"I know I can't sit here alive and safe and talk about falling down some stairs when all that terror, all those dead."

He didn't interrupt. He let her talk and didn't try to reassure her. What was there to be reassuring about? She was slumped in the chair now, talking into the tabletop.

"The firemen racing past. And asthma, asthma. And some people talking said bomb. They were trying to talk on cell phones. They went down the stairs hitting numbers."

This is where bottles of water were passed up the line from somewhere below, and soft drinks, and people were even joking a little, the equity traders.

This is where the firemen went racing past, going up the stairs, into it, and people got out of the way.

This is also where she saw someone she knew, going up, a maintenance man, a guy she used to joke with whenever she saw him, going up right past her, carrying a long iron implement, like something to pry open an elevator door, maybe, and she tried to think of the word for the thing.

He waited. She looked past him, thinking, and it seemed important to her, as if she were trying to recall the man's name, not the name of the tool he was carrying.

Finally he said, "Crowbar."

"Crowbar," she said, thinking about it, seeing it again.

Keith thought he'd also seen the man, going up past him, a guy in a hard hat and wearing a workbelt with tools and flashlights and carrying a crowbar, bent end first.

No reason ever to remember this if she hadn't mentioned it. Means nothing, he thought. But then it did. Whatever had happened to the man was situated outside the fact that they'd both seen him, at different points in the march down, but it was important, somehow, in some indeterminate way, that he'd been carried in these crossing memories, brought down out of the tower and into this room.

He leaned forward, elbow braced on the coffee table, mouth pressed against his hand, and he watched her.

"We just kept going down. Dark, light, dark again. I feel like I'm still on the stairs. I wanted my mother. If I live to be a hundred I'll still be on the stairs. It took so long it was almost normal in a way. We couldn't run so it wasn't some kind of running frenzy. We were stuck together. I wanted my mother. This ain't no earthquake, making ten million dollars a year."

They were moving out of the worst of the smoke now and this is when she saw the dog, a blind man and a guide dog, not far ahead, and it was like something out of the Bible, she thought. They seemed so calm. They seemed to spread calm, she thought. The dog was like some totally calming thing. They believed in the dog.

"We, finally, I don't know how long we had to wait, it was dark wherever we were but then we came out and passed some windows and saw the plaza where it's a bombed-out city, things on fire, we saw bodies, we saw clothes, pieces of metal like metal parts, things just scattered. This was like two seconds. I looked two seconds and looked away and then we went through the underground concourse and up into the street."

This was all she said for a time. He went over to the chair by the door and found her cigarettes in the briefcase and took one out of the pack and put it in his mouth and then found the lighter.

"In the smoke all I could see was those stripes on the firemen's coats, the bright stripes, and then some people in the rubble, all that steel and glass, just injured people sitting dreaming, they were like dreamers bleeding."

She turned and looked at him. He lit the cigarette and walked over and handed it to her. She took a drag, closing her eyes and exhaling. When she looked again, he was back across the table, seated on the sofa, watching her.

"Light one up for yourself," she said.

"Not for me, no."

"You quit."

"Long time ago. When I thought I was an athlete," he said. "But blow some my way. That would be nice."

After a while she began to speak again. But he didn't know where she was, somewhere back near the beginning, he thought.

He thought, Wet all through. She was wet all through.

There were people everywhere pushing into the stairwell. She tried to recall things and faces, moments that might explain something or reveal something. She believed in the guide dog. The dog would lead them all to safety.

She was going through it again and he was ready to listen again. He listened carefully, noting every detail, trying to find himself in the crowd.

Her mother had said it clearly, years earlier.

"There's a certain man, an archetype, he's a model of dependability for his male friends, all the things a friend should be, an ally and confidant, lends money, gives advice, loyal and so on, but sheer hell on women. Living breathing hell. The closer a woman gets, the clearer it becomes to him that she is not one of his male friends. And the more awful it becomes for her. This is Keith. This is the man you're going to marry."

This is the man she marries.

He was a hovering presence now. There drifted through the rooms a sense of someone who has earned respectful attention. He was not quite returned to his body yet. Even the program of exercises he did for his postsurgical wrist seemed a little detached, four times a day, an odd set of extensions and flexions that resembled prayer in some remote northern province, among a repressed people, with periodic applications of ice. He spent time with Justin, taking him to school and picking him up, advising on homework. He wore a splint for a while, then stopped. He took the kid to the park to play catch. The kid could toss a baseball all day and be purely and inexhaustibly happy, unmarked by sin, anyone's, down the ages. Throw and catch. She watched them in a field not far from the museum, into the sinking sun. When Keith did a kind of ball trick, using the right hand, the undamaged one, to flip the ball onto the back of the hand and then jerk the arm forward propelling the ball backwards along the forearm before knocking it into the air with his elbow and then catching it backhanded, she saw a man she'd never known before.

She stopped at Harold Apter's office in the East 80s on her way to 116th Street. She did this periodically, dropping off photocopies of her group's written pieces and discussing their situations in general. This is where Dr. Apter saw people for consultation, Alzheimer patients and others.

Apter was a slight man with frizzed hair who seemed formulated to say funny things but never did. They talked about the fade of Rosellen S., the aloof bearing of Curtis B. She told him she would like to increase the frequency of the meetings to twice a week. He told her this would be a mistake.

"From this point on, you understand, it's all about loss. We're dealing inevitably here with diminishing returns. Their situation will grow increasingly delicate. These encounters need space around them. You don't want them to feel there's an urgency to write everything, say everything before it's too late. You want them to look forward to this, not feel pressed or threatened. The writing is sweet music up to a point. Then other things will take over."

He looked at her searchingly.

"What I'm saying is simple. This is for them," he said.

"What do you mean?"

"It's theirs," he said. "Don't make it yours."

They wrote about the planes. They wrote about where they were when it happened. They wrote about people they knew who were in the towers, or nearby, and they wrote about God.

How could God let this happen? Where was God when this happened?

Benny T. was glad he was not a man of faith because he would lose it after this.

I am closer to God than ever, Rosellen wrote.

This is the devil. This is hell. All that fire and pain. Never mind God. This is hell.

Omar H. was afraid to go out on the street in the days after. They were looking at him, he thought.

I didn't see them holding hands. I wanted to see that, Rosellen wrote.

Carmen G. wanted to know whether everything that happens to us has to be part of God's plan.

I am closer to God than ever, am closer, will be closer, shall be closer.

Eugene A., in a rare appearance, wrote that God knows things we don't know.

Ashes and bones. That's what's left of God's plan.

But when the towers fell, Omar wrote.

I keep hearing they were holding hands when they jumped.

If God let this happen, with the planes, then did God make me cut my finger when I was slicing bread this morning?

They wrote and then read what they'd written, each in turn, and there were remarks and then exchanges and then monologues.

"Show us the finger," Benny said. "We want to kiss it."

Lianne encouraged them to speak and argue. She wanted to hear everything, the things everybody said, ordinary things, and the naked statements of belief, and the depth of feeling, the passion that saturated the room. She needed these men and women. Dr. Apter's comment disturbed her because there was truth in it. She needed these people. It was possible that the group meant more to her than it did to the members. There was something precious here, something that seeps and bleeds. These people were the living breath of the thing that killed her father.

"God says something happens, then it happens."

"I don't respect God no more, after this."

"We sit and listen and God tells us or doesn't."

"I was walking down the street to get my hair cut. Somebody comes running."

"I was on the crapper. I hated myself later. People said where were you when it happened. I didn't tell them where I was."

"But you remember to tell us. That's beautiful, Benny."

They interrupted, gestured, changed the subject, talked over each other, shut their eyes in thought or puzzlement or in dismal re-experience of the event itself.

"What about the people God saved? Are they better people than the ones who died?"

"It's not ours to ask. We don't ask."

"A million babies die in Africa and we can't ask."

"I thought it was war. I thought it was war," Anna said. "I stayed inside and lit a candle. It's the Chinese, my sister said, who she never trusted with the bomb."

Lianne struggled with the idea of God. She was taught to believe that religion makes people compliant. This is the purpose of religion, to return people to a childlike state. Awe and submission, her mother said. This is why religion speaks so powerfully in laws, rituals and punishments. And it speaks beautifully as well, inspiring music and art, elevating consciousness in some, reducing it in others. People fall into trances, people literally go to the ground, people crawl great distances or march in crowds stabbing themselves and whipping themselves. And other people, the rest of us, maybe we're rocked more gently, joined to something deep in the soul. Powerful and beautiful, her mother said. We want to transcend, we want to pass beyond the limits of safe understanding, and what better way to do it than through make-believe.

Eugene A. was seventy-seven years old, hair gelled and spiked, a ring in his ear.

"I was scrubbing the sink for once in my life when the phone rings. It's my ex-wife," he said, "that I haven't talked to in like seventeen years, is she even alive or dead, calling from somewhere I can't even pronounce it, in Florida. I say what. She says never mind what. That same voice of no respect. She says turn on TV."

"I had to watch at a neighbor," Omar said.

"Seventeen years, not one word. Look what has to happen before she finally gets it in her head to call. Turn on TV, she tells me."

The cross talk continued.

"I don't forgive God what He did."

"How do you explain this to a child whose mother or father?"

"You lie to children."

"I wanted to see that, the ones that were holding hands."

"When you see something happening, it's supposed to be real."

"But God. Did God do this or not?"

"You're looking right at it. But it's not really happening."

"He has the big things that He does. He shakes the world," said Curtis B.

"I would say to someone at least he didn't die with a tube in his stomach or wearing a bag for his waste."

"Ashes and bones."

"I am closer to God, I know it, we know it, they know it."

"This is our prayer room," Omar said.

No one wrote a word about the terrorists. And in the exchanges that followed the readings, no one spoke about the terrorists. She prompted them. There has to be something you want to say, some feeling to express, nineteen men come here to kill us.

She waited, not certain what it was she wanted to hear. Then Anna C. mentioned a man she knew, a fireman, lost in one of the towers.

All along Anna had been slightly apart, interjecting only once or twice, matter-of-factly. Now she used hand gestures to help direct her story, sitting hard and squat in a flimsy folding chair, and no one interrupted.

"If he has a heart attack, we blame him. Eats, overeats, no exercise, no common sense. That's what I told the wife. Or he dies of cancer. Smoked and couldn't stop. That was Mike. If it's cancer, then it's lung cancer and we blame him. But this, what happened, it's way too big, it's outside someplace, on the other side of the world. You can't get to these people or even see them in their pictures in the paper. You can see their faces but what does it mean? Means nothing to call them names. I'm a name-caller from before I was born. Do I know what to call these people?"

Lianne suspected what this was. It was a response defined in terms of revenge and she welcomed this, the small intimate wish, however useless in a hellstorm.

"He dies in a car crash or walking across the street, hit by a car, you can kill the person in your mind a thousand times, the driver. You couldn't do the actual thing, in all honesty, because you don't have the wherewithal, but you could think it, you could see it in your mind and get some trade-off from that. But here, with these people, you can't even think it. You don't know what to do. Because they're a million miles outside your life. Which, besides, they're dead."

There was religion, then there was God. Lianne wanted to

disbelieve. Disbelief was the line of travel that led to clarity of thought and purpose. Or was this simply another form of superstition? She wanted to trust in the forces and processes of the natural world, this only, perceptible reality and scientific endeavor, men and women alone on earth. She knew there was no conflict between science and God. Take one with the other. But she didn't want to. There were the scholars and philosophers she'd studied in school, books she'd read as thrilling dispatches, personal, making her shake at times, and there was the sacred art she'd always loved. Doubters created this work, and ardent believers, and those who'd doubted and then believed, and she was free to think and doubt and believe simultaneously. But she didn't want to. God would crowd her, make her weaker. God would be a presence that remained unimaginable. She wanted this only, to snuff out the pulse of the shaky faith she'd held for much of her life.

He began to think into the day, into the minute. It was being here, alone in time, that made this happen, being away from routine stimulus, all the streaming forms of office discourse. Things seemed still, they seemed clearer to the eye, oddly, in ways he didn't understand. He began to see what he was doing. He noticed things, all the small lost strokes of a day or a minute, how he licked his thumb and used it to lift a bread crumb off the plate and put it idly in his mouth. Only it wasn't so idle anymore. Nothing seemed familiar, being here, in a family again, and he felt strange to himself, or always had, but it was different now because he was watching.

There were the walks to school with Justin and the walks back home, alone, or somewhere else, just walking, and then he picked up the kid at school and it was back home again. There was a contained elation in these times, a feeling that was nearly hidden, something he knew but only barely, a whisper of self-disclosure.

The kid was trying to speak in monosyllables only, for extended stretches. This was something his class was doing, a serious game designed to teach the children something about the structure of words and the discipline required to frame clear thoughts. Lianne said, half seriously, that it sounded totalitarian.

"It helps me go slow when I think," Justin said to his father, measuring each word, noting the syllable count.

It was Keith as well who was going slow, easing inward. He used to want to fly out of self-awareness, day and night, a body in raw motion. Now he finds himself drifting into spells of reflection, thinking not in clear units, hard and linked, but only absorbing what comes, drawing things out of time and memory and into some dim space that bears his collected experience. Or he stands and looks. He stands at the window and sees what's happening in the street. Something is always happening, even on the quietest days and deep into night, if you stand a while and look.

He thought of something out of nowhere, a phrase, *organic shrapnel*. Felt familiar but meant nothing to him. Then he saw a car double-parked across the street and thought of something else and then something else again.

There were the walks to and from school, the meals he cooked, something he'd rarely done in the past year and a half because it made him feel like the last man alive, breaking eggs for dinner. There was the park, every kind of weather, and there was the woman who lived across the park. But that was another matter, the walk across the park.

"We go home now," Justin said.

She was awake, middle of the night, eyes closed, mind running, and she felt time pressing in, and threat, a kind of beat in her head.

She read everything they wrote about the attacks.

She thought of her father. She saw him coming down an escalator, in an airport maybe.

Keith stopped shaving for a time, whatever that means. Everything seemed to mean something. Their lives were in transition and she looked for signs. Even when she was barely aware of an incident it came to mind later, with meaning attached, in sleepless episodes that lasted minutes or hours, she wasn't sure.

They lived on the top floor of a redbrick building, four-storied, and often now, these past days, she walked down the stairs and heard a certain kind of music, wailing music, lutes and tambourines and chanting voices sometimes, coming from the apartment on the second floor, the same CD, she thought, over and over, and it was beginning to make her angry.

She read stories in newspapers until she had to force herself to stop.

But things were ordinary as well. Things were ordinary in all the ways they were always ordinary.

A woman named Elena lived in that apartment. Maybe Elena was Greek, she thought. But the music wasn't Greek. She was hearing another set of traditions, Middle Eastern, North African, Bedouin songs perhaps or Sufi dances, music located in Islamic tradition, and she thought of knocking on the door and saying something.

She told people she wanted to leave the city. They knew she wasn't serious and said so and she hated them a little, and her own transparency, and the small panics that made certain moments in the waking day resemble the frantic ramblings of this very time of night, the mind ever running.

She thought of her father. She carried her father's name. She was Lianne Glenn. Her father had been a traditional lapsed Catholic, devoted to the Latin mass as long as he didn't have to sit through it. He made no distinction between Catholics and lapsed Catholics. The only thing that mattered was tradition but not in his work, never there, his designs for buildings and other structures, situated in mostly remote landscapes.

She thought she might adopt a posture of fake civility, as a tactic, a means of answering one offense with another. They heard it mainly on the stairs, Keith said, going up and down, and it's only music anyway, he said, so why not just forget it.

They didn't own, they rented, like people in the Middle Ages.

She wanted to knock on the door and say something to Elena. Ask her what the point is. Adopt a posture. This is retaliation in itself. Ask her why she's playing this particular music at this highly sensitive time. Use the language of the concerned fellow tenant.

She read newspaper profiles of the dead.

When she was a girl she wanted to be her mother, her father, certain of her schoolmates, one or two, who seemed to move with particular ease, to say things that didn't matter except in the way they were said, on an easy breeze, like birdflight. She slept with one of these girls, they touched a little and kissed once and she thought of this as a dream she would wake from in the mind and body of the other girl.

Knock on the door. Mention the noise. Don't call it music, call it noise.

They're the ones who think alike, talk alike, eat the same food at the same time. She knew this wasn't true. Say the same prayers, word for word, in the same prayer stance, day and night, following the arc of sun and moon.

She needed to sleep now. She needed to stop the noise in

her head and turn on her right side, toward her husband, and breathe his air and sleep his sleep.

Elena was either an office manager or a restaurant manager, and divorced, and living with a large dog, and who knew what else.

She liked his facial hair, the hair was okay, but she didn't say anything. She said one thing, uninteresting, and watched him run his thumb over the stubble, marking its presence for himself.

They said, Leave the city? For what? To go where? It was the locally honed cosmocentric idiom of New York, loud and blunt, but she felt it in her heart no less than they did.

Do this. Knock on the door. Adopt a posture. Mention the noise as noise. Knock on the door, mention the noise, use the open pretense of civility and calm, the parody of fellow-tenant courtesy that every tenant sees as such, and gently mention the noise. But mention the noise only as noise. Knock on the door, mention the noise, adopt a posture of suave calm, openly phony, and do not allude to the underlying theme of a certain kind of music as a certain form of political and religious statement, now of all times. Work gradually into the language of aggrieved tenancy. Ask her if she rents or owns.

She turned on her right side, toward her husband, and opened her eyes.

Thoughts from nowhere, elsewhere, someone else's.

She opened her eyes and was surprised, even now, to see him there in bed, next to her, a flat surprise by this time, fifteen days after the planes. They'd made love in the night, earlier, she wasn't sure when, two or three hours ago. It was back there somewhere, a laying open of bodies but also of time, the only interval she'd known in these days and nights that was not forced or distorted, hemmed in by the press of events. It was the tenderest sex she'd known with him. She felt some drool at the corner of her mouth, the part that was mashed into the pillow, and she watched him, faceup, head in distinct profile against the wan light from the streetlamp.

She'd never felt easy with that term. My husband. He wasn't a husband. The word spouse had seemed comical, applied to him, and husband simply didn't fit. He was something else somewhere else. But now she uses the term. She believes he is growing into it, a husbandman, even though she knows this is another word completely.

What is already in the air, in the bodies of the young, and what is next to come.

The music included moments of what sounded like forced breathing. She heard it on the stairs one day, an interlude consisting of men breathing in urgent rhythmic pattern, a liturgy of inhale-exhale, and other voices at other times, trance voices, voices in recitation, women in devotional lament, mingled village voices behind hand drums and hand claps.

She watched her husband, face empty of expression, neutral, not very different from his waking aspect.

All right the music is beautiful but why now, what's the particular point of this, and what's the name of the thing like a lute that's played with an eagle's quill.

She reached a hand to his beating chest.

Time, finally, to go to sleep, following the arc of sun and moon.

She was back from an early-morning run and stood sweating by the kitchen window, drinking water from a one-liter bottle and watching Keith eat breakfast.

"You're one of those madwomen running in the streets. Run around the reservoir."

"You think we look crazier than men."

"Only in the streets."

"I like the streets. This time of morning, there's something about the city, down by the river, streets nearly empty, cars blasting by on the Drive."

"Breathe deeply."

"I like running alongside the cars on the Drive."

"Take deep breaths," he said. "Let the fumes swirl into your lungs."

"I like the fumes. I like the breeze from the river."

"Run naked," he said.

"You do it, I'll do it."

"I'll do it if the kid does it," he said.

Justin was in his room, a Saturday, putting last touches, last pokes of color onto a portrait he'd been doing, in crayon, of his grandmother. Either that or drawing a picture of a bird, for school, which reminded her of something.

"He takes the binoculars over to the Siblings'. Any idea why?"

"They're searching the skies."

"For what?"

"Planes. One of them, I think it was the girl."

"Katie."

"Katie claims she saw the plane that hit Tower One. She says she was home from school, sick, standing at the window when the plane flew by."

The building where the Siblings lived was known to some as Godzilla Apartments or simply the Godzilla. It was forty stories or so in an area of town houses and other structures of modest height and it created its own weather systems, with strong currents of air sometimes shearing down the face of the building and knocking old people to the pavement.

"Home sick. Do I believe that?"

"I think they're on the twenty-seventh floor," he said.

"Looking west across the park. This much is true."

"Did the plane fly down over the park?"

"Maybe the park, maybe the river," she said. "And maybe she was home sick and maybe she made it up."

"Either way."

"Either way, you're saying, they're looking for more planes."

"Waiting for it to happen again."

"That scares me," she said.

"This time with a pair of binoculars to help them make the sighting."

"That scares the hell out of me. God, there's something so awful about that. Damn kids with their goddamn twisted powers of imagination."

She walked over to the table and picked half a strawberry out of his cereal bowl. Then she sat across from him, thinking and chewing.

Finally she said, "The only thing I got out of Justin. The towers did not collapse."

"I told him they did."

"So did I," she said.

"They were hit but did not collapse. That's what he says."

"He didn't see it on TV. I didn't want him to see it. But I told him they came down. And he seemed to absorb it. But then, I don't know."

"He knows they came down, whatever he says about it."

"He has to know, don't you think? And he knows you were there."

"We talked about it," Keith said. "But only once."

"What did he say?"

"Not much. And neither did I."

"They're searching the skies."

"That's right," he said.

She knew there was something she'd wanted to say all along and it finally seeped into wordable awareness.

"Has he said anything about this man Bill Lawton?"

"Just once. He wasn't supposed to tell anyone."

"Their mother mentioned this name. I keep forgetting to tell you. First I forget the name. I forget the easy names. Then, when I remember, you're never around to tell."

"The kid slipped. He let the name slip. He told me the planes were a secret. I'm not supposed to tell anyone the three of them are up there on the twenty-seventh floor searching the skies. But mostly, he said, I'm not supposed to mention Bill Lawton. Then he realized what he'd done. He'd let the name slip. And he wanted me to give him double and triple promises. No one's allowed to know."

"Including his mother who gave birth to him in four and a half hours of blood and pain. This is why women go running through the streets."

"Amen. But what happened," he said, "is that the other kid, the little brother."

"Robert."

"The name originates with Robert. This much I know. The rest I mostly surmise. Robert thought, from television or school or somewhere, that he was hearing a certain name. Maybe he heard the name once, or misheard it, then imposed this version on future occasions. In other words he never adjusted his original sense of what he was hearing."

"What was he hearing?"

"He was hearing Bill Lawton. They were saying bin Laden."

Lianne considered this. It seemed to her, at first, that some important meaning might be located in the soundings of the boy's small error. She looked at Keith, searching for his concurrence, for something she might use to secure her free-floating awe. He chewed his food and shrugged.

"So, together," he said, "they developed the myth of Bill Lawton."

"Katie's got to know the real name. She's way too smart. She probably keeps the other name going precisely because it's the wrong name."

"I guess that's the idea. That's the myth."

"Bill Lawton."

"Searching the skies for Bill Lawton. He told me some things before he clammed up."

"One thing I like. I like knowing the answer to the riddle before Isabel knows."

"Who's that?"

"The Siblings' mother."

"What about *her* blood and pain?"

She laughed at that. But the thought of them at the window, with the door closed, searching the skies, continued to disturb her.

"Bill Lawton has a long beard. He wears a long robe," he said. "He flies jet planes and speaks thirteen languages but not English except to his wives. What else? He has the power to poison what we eat but only certain foods. They're working on the list."

"This is what we get for putting a protective distance between children and news events."

"Except we didn't put a distance, not really," he said.

"Between children and mass murderers."

"The other thing he does, Bill Lawton, is go everywhere in his bare feet."

"They killed your best friend. They're fucking outright murderers. Two friends, two friends."

"I talked to Demetrius a little while ago. I don't think you met him. Worked in the other tower. They sent him to a burn unit in Baltimore. He has family there."

She looked at him.

"Why are you still here?"

She said this in a tone of gentlest curiosity.

"Are you planning to stay? Because I think this is something we need to talk about," she said. "I've forgotten how to talk to you. This is the longest talk we've had."

"You did it better than anybody. Talk to me. Maybe that was the problem."

"I guess I've unlearned it. Because I sit here thinking we have so much to say."

"We don't have so much to say. We used to say everything, all the time. We examined everything, all the questions, all the issues."

"All right."

"It practically killed us."

"All right. But is it possible? Here's my question," she said. "Is it possible you and I are done with conflict? You know what I mean. The everyday friction. The every-word every-breath schedule we were on before we split. Is it possible this is over? We don't need this anymore. We can live without it. Am I right?"

"We're ready to sink into our little lives," he said.

They stood in the entranceway watching the cold rain fall, younger man and older, after evening prayer. The wind sent trash skidding along the sidewalk and Hammad cupped his hands to his mouth and exhaled six or seven times, slowly and deliberately, feeling a whisper of warm breath on his palms. A woman on a bike went past, pedaling hard. He crossed his arms on his chest now, hands buried in armpits, and he listened to the older man's story.

He was a rifleman in the Shatt al Arab, fifteen years ago, watching them come across the mudflats, thousands of shouting boys. Some carried rifles, many did not, and the weapons nearly overwhelmed the smaller boys, Kalashnikovs, too heavy to be carried very far. He was a soldier in Saddam's army and they were the martyrs of the Ayatollah, here to fall and die. They seemed to come up out of the wet earth, wave on wave, and he aimed and fired and watched them fall. He was flanked by machine-gun positions and the firing grew so intense he began to think he was breathing white-hot steel.

Hammad barely knew this man, a baker, here in Hamburg maybe ten years. They prayed in the same mosque, this is what he knew, on the second floor of this shabby building with graffiti smeared on the outer walls and a setting of local strolling whores. Now he knew this as well, the face of combat in the long war.

The boys kept coming and the machine guns cut them down. After a time the man understood there was no point shooting anymore, not for him. Even if they were the enemy, Iranians, Shiites, heretics, this was not for him, watching them vault the smoking bodies of their brothers, carrying their souls in their hands. The other thing he understood is that this was a military tactic, ten thousand boys enacting the glory of self-sacrifice to divert Iraqi troops and equipment from the real army massing behind front lines.

Most countries are run by madmen, he said.

Then he said he was twice regretful, first to see the boys die, sent out to explode land mines and to run under tanks and into walls of gunfire, and then to think they were winning, these children, defeating us in the manner of their dying.

Hammad listened without comment but was grateful to the man. He was the kind of man who is not old yet by strict count but who carries something heavier than hard years.

But the shouts of the boys, the high-pitched cry. The man said this is what he heard above the noise of battle. The boys were sounding the cry of history, the story of ancient Shia defeat and the allegiance of the living to those who were dead and defeated. That cry is still close to me, he said. Not like something happening yesterday but something always happening, over a thousand years happening, always in the air.

Hammad stood nodding. He felt the cold in his bones, the misery of wet winds and northern nights. They stood in silence for a time, waiting for the rain to stop, and he kept thinking that another woman would come by on a bike, someone to look at, hair wet, legs pumping.

They were all growing beards. One of them even told his father to grow a beard. Men came to the flat on Marienstrasse, some to visit, others to live, men in and out all the time, growing beards.

Hammad sat crouched, eating and listening. The talk was fire and light, the emotion contagious. They were in this country to pursue technical educations but in these rooms they spoke about the struggle. Everything here was twisted, hypocrite, the West corrupt of mind and body, determined to shiver Islam down to bread crumbs for birds.

They studied architecture and engineering. They studied urban planning and one of them blamed the Jews for defects in construction. The Jews build walls too thin, aisles too narrow. The Jews built the toilet in this flat too close to the floor so a man's stream of liquid leaves his body and travels so far it makes a noise and a splash, which people in the next room can sit and listen to. Thanks to the thin Jew walls.

Hammad wasn't sure whether this was funny, true or stupid. He listened to everything they said, intently. He was a bulky man, clumsy, and thought all his life that some unnamed energy was sealed in his body, too tight to be released.

He didn't know which one of them had told his father to grow a beard. Tell your father to grow a beard. This is not normally recommended.

The man who led discussions, this was Amir and he was intense, a small thin wiry man who spoke to Hammad in his face. He was very genius, others said, and he told them that a man can stay forever in a room, doing blueprints, eating and sleeping, even praying, even plotting, but at a certain point he has to get out. Even if the room is a place of prayer, he can't stay there all his life. Islam is the world outside the prayer room as well as the *sūrahs* in the Koran. Islam is the struggle against the enemy, near enemy and far, Jews first, for all things unjust and hateful, and then the Americans.

They needed space of their own, in the mosque, in the portable prayer room at the university, here in the apartment on Marien-strasse.

There were seven pairs of shoes set outside the door of the flat. Hammad went in and they were talking and arguing. One of the men had fought in Bosnia, another avoided contact with dogs and women.

They looked at videos of jihad in other countries and Hammad told them about the boy soldiers running in the mud, the mine jumpers, wearing keys to paradise around their necks. They stared him down, they talked him down. That was a long time ago and those were only boys, they said, not worth the time it would take to be sorry for a single one.

Late one night he had to step over the prone form of a brother in prayer as he made his way to the toilet to jerk off.

The world changes first in the mind of the man who wants to change it. The time is coming, our truth, our shame, and each man becomes the other, and the other still another, and then there is no separation.

Amir spoke in his face. His full name was Mohamed Mohamed el-Amir el-Sayed Atta.

There was the feeling of lost history. They were too long in isolation. This is what they talked about, being crowded out by other cultures, other futures, the all-enfolding will of capital markets and foreign policies.

This was Amir, his mind was in the upper skies, making sense of things, drawing things together.

Hammad knew a woman who was German, Syrian, what else, a little Turkish. She had dark eyes and a floppy body that liked contact. They shuffled across the room toward her cot, clamped tight, with her roommate on the other side of the door studying English. Everything happened in crowded segments of place and time. His dreams seemed compressed, small rooms, nearly bare, quickly dreamt. Sometimes he and the two women played crude word games, inventing nonsense rhymes in four pidgin languages.

He didn't know the name of the German security agency in any language. Some of the men who passed through the flat were dangerous to the state. Read the texts, fire the guns. They were probably being watched, phones tapped, signals intercepted. They preferred anyway to talk in person. They knew that all signals traveling in the air are vulnerable to interception. The state has microwave sites. The state has ground stations and floating satellites, Internet exchange points. There is photo reconnaissance that takes a picture of a dung beetle from one hundred kilometers up.

But we encounter face to face. A man turns up from Kandahar, another from Riyadh. We encounter directly, in the flat or in the mosque. The state has fiber optics but power is helpless against us. The more power, the more helpless. We encounter through eyes, through word and look.

Hammad and two others went looking for a man on the Reeperbahn. It was late and bitter cold and they saw him finally coming out of a house half a block away. One of the men called his name, then the other. He looked at them and waited and Hammad advanced and hit him three or four times and he went down. The other men advanced and kicked him. Hammad hadn't known his name until they shouted it out and he wasn't sure what this was all about, the guy paying an Albanian whore for sex or the guy not growing a beard. He had no beard, Hammad noticed, just before he hit him.

They ate skewered meat in a Turkish restaurant. He showed her the dimensional specifications he did in class, where he studied mechanical drawing, halfheartedly. He felt more intelligent when he was with her because she encouraged exactly this, asking questions or just being herself, being curious about things including his friends at the mosque. His friends gave him a reason to be mysterious, a circumstance she found interesting. Her roommate listened to cool voices speaking English in her headset. Hammad troubled her for lessons, for words and phrases and we can skip the grammar. There was a rush, a pull that made it hard to see beyond the minute. He flew through the minutes and felt the draw of some huge future landscape opening up, all mountain and sky.

He spent time at the mirror looking at his beard, knowing he was not supposed to trim it.

He did a little lusting after the roommate when he saw her ride her bike but tried not to bring this craving into the house. His girlfriend clung to him and they did damage to the cot. She wanted him to know her whole presence, inside and out. They ate falafel wrapped in pita and sometimes he wanted to marry her and have babies but this was only in the minutes after he left her flat, feeling like a footballer running across the field after scoring a goal, all-world, his arms flung wide.

The time is coming.

The men went to Internet cafés and learned about flight schools in the United States. Nobody knocked down their door in the middle of the night and nobody stopped them in the street to turn their pockets inside out and grope their bodies for weapons. But they knew that Islam was under attack.

Amir looked at him, seeing right down to his base self. Hammad knew what he would say. Eating all the time, pushing food in your face, slow to approach your prayers. There was more. Being with a shameless woman, dragging your body over hers. What is the difference between you and all the others, outside our space?

When Amir spoke the words, talking in his face, he inflected them with sarcasm.

Am I talking Chinese? Do I stutter? Are my lips moving but no words come?

Hammad in a certain way thought this was unfair. But the closer he examined himself, the truer the words. He had to fight against the need to be normal. He had to struggle against himself, first, and then against the injustice that haunted their lives.

They read the sword verses of the Koran. They were strong-willed, determined to become one mind. Shed everything but the men you are with. Become each other's running blood.

Sometimes there were ten pairs of shoes outside the door of the flat, eleven pairs of shoes. This was the house of the followers, that's what they called it, *dar al-ansar*, and that's what they were, followers of the Prophet.

The beard would look better if he trimmed it. But there were rules now and he was determined to follow them. His life had structure. Things were clearly defined. He was becoming one of them now, learning to look like them and think like them. This was inseparable from jihad. He prayed with them to be with them. They were becoming total brothers.

The woman's name was Leyla. Pretty eyes and knowing touch. He told her that he was going away for a time, absolutely to return. Soon she would begin to exist as an unreliable memory, then finally not at all.

PART TWO

ERNST HECHINGER

6

When he appeared at the door it was not possible, a man come out of an ash storm, all blood and slag, reeking of burnt matter, with pinpoint glints of slivered glass in his face. He looked immense, in the doorway, with a gaze that had no focus in it. He carried a briefcase and stood slowly nodding. She thought he might be in shock but didn't know what this meant in precise terms, medical terms. He walked past her toward the kitchen and she tried calling her doctor, then 911, then the nearest hospital, but all she heard was the drone of overloaded lines. She turned off the TV set, not sure why, protecting him from the news he'd just walked out of, that's why, and then went into the kitchen. He was sitting at the table and she poured him a glass of water and told him that Justin was with his grandmother, released early from school and also being protected from the news, at least as it concerned his father.

He said, "Everybody's giving me water."

She thought he could not have traveled all this distance or even climbed the stairs if he'd suffered serious injury, grievous blood loss.

Then he said something else. The briefcase sat beside the

table like something yanked out of a landfill. He said there was a shirt coming down out of the sky.

She poured water on a dishcloth and wiped dust and ash from his hands, face and head, careful not to disturb the glass fragments. There was more blood than she'd realized at first and then she began to realize something else, that his cuts and abrasions were not severe enough or numerous enough to account for all this blood. It was not his blood. Most of it came from somebody else.

The windows were open so Florence could smoke. They sat where they'd sat last time, one on either side of the coffee table, positioned diagonally.

"I gave myself a year," he said.

"An actor. I can see you as an actor."

"Acting student. Never got beyond the student part."

"Because there's something about you, in the way you hold a space. I'm not sure what that means."

"Sounds good."

"I think I heard it somewhere. What does it mean?" she said.

"Gave myself a year. I thought it would be interesting. Cut it to six months. I thought, What else can I do? I played two sports in college. That was over. Six months, what the hell. Cut it to four, was gone in two."

She studied him, she sat there and stared, and there was something about this, such frank and innocent openness of manner that he stopped feeling unnerved after a while. She looked, they talked, here in a room he would not have been able to describe a minute after leaving.

"Didn't work out. Things don't work out," she said. "What did you do?"

"Went to law school."

She whispered, "Why?"

"What else? Where else?"

She sat back and put the cigarette to her lips, thinking about something. There were small brown specks on her face spilling from the lower forehead down onto the bridge of the nose.

"You're married, I guess. Not that I care."

"Yes, I am."

"I don't care," she said, and it was the first time he'd heard resentment in her voice.

"We were apart, now we're back, or beginning to be back."

"Of course," she said.

This was the second time he'd walked across the park. He knew why he was here but could not have explained it to someone and did not have to explain it to her. It didn't matter whether they spoke or not. It would be fine, not speaking, breathing the same air, or she speaks, he listens, or day is night.

She said, "I went to St. Paul's yesterday. I wanted to be with people, down there in particular. I knew there would be people there. I looked at the flowers and the personal things people left, the homemade memorials. I didn't look at the photographs of the missing. I couldn't do that. I sat in the chapel for an hour and people came in and prayed or just walked around, only looking, reading the marble plaques. In memory of, in memory of. Rescue workers came in, three of them, and I tried not to stare, and then two more came in."

She'd been married for a brief time, ten years earlier, a mistake so fleeting it left few marks. That's what she said. The man died some months after the marriage ended, in a car crash, and his mother blamed Florence. That was the mark it left.

"I say to myself dying is ordinary."

"Not when it's you. Not when it's someone you know."

"I'm not saying we shouldn't grieve. Just, why don't we put it in God's hands?" she said. "Why haven't we learned this, after all the evidence of all the dead? We're supposed to believe in God but then why don't we obey the laws of God's universe, which teach us how small we are and where we're all going to end up?"

"Can't be that simple."

"Those men who did this thing. They're anti everything we stand for. But they believe in God," she said.

"Whose God? Which God? I don't even know what it means, to believe in God. I never think about it."

"Never think about it."

"Does that upset you?"

"It frightens me," she said. "I've always felt the presence of God. I talk to God sometimes. I don't have to be in church to talk to God. I go to church but not, you know, week in, week out—what's the word I'm thinking of?"

"Religiously," he said.

He could make her laugh. She seemed to look into him when she laughed, eyes alive, seeing something he could not guess at. There was an element in Florence that was always close to some emotional distress, a memory of bearing injury or sustaining loss, possibly lifelong, and the laughter was a kind of shedding, a physical deliverance from old woe, dead skin, if only for a moment.

There was music coming from a back room, something classical and familiar but he didn't know the name of the piece or the composer. He never knew these things. They drank tea and talked. She talked about the tower, going over it again, claustrophobically, the smoke, the fold of bodies, and he understood that they could talk about these things only with each other, in minute and dullest detail, but it would never be dull or too detailed because it was inside them now and because he needed to hear what he'd lost in the tracings of memory. This was their pitch of delirium, the dazed reality they'd shared in the stairwells, the deep shafts of spiraling men and women.

The talk continued, touching on marriage, friendship, the future. He was an amateur at this but spoke willingly enough. Mostly he listened.

"What we carry. This is the story in the end," she said remotely.

His car hit a wall. His mother blamed Florence because if they'd still been married he wouldn't have been in that car on that road and since she was the one who'd ended the marriage the blame was hers, the mark was hers.

"He was an older man by seventeen years. It sounds so tragic. An older man. He had an engineering degree but worked in the post office."

"He drank."

"Yes."

"He was drinking the night of the crash."

"Yes. It was afternoon. Broad daylight. No other cars involved."

He told her it was time for him to leave.

"Of course. You have to. That's the way these things happen. Everybody knows that."

She seemed to be blaming him for this, the fact of leaving, the fact of marrying, the thoughtless gesture of reuniting, and at the same time did not seem to be talking to him at all. She was talking to the room, to herself, he thought, talking back in time to some version of herself, a person who might confirm the grim familiarity of the moment. She wanted her feelings to register, officially, and needed to say the actual words, if not necessarily to him.

But he remained in the chair.

He said, "What is that music?"

"I think I need to make it go away. It's like movie music in those old movies when the man and woman run through the heather."

"Tell the truth. You love those movies."

"I love the music too. But only when it's playing in the movie."

She looked at him and got up. She went past the front door and down the hall. She was plain except when she laughed. She was someone on the subway. She wore loose skirts and plain shoes and was full-figured and maybe a little clumsy but when she laughed there was a flare in nature, an unfolding of something half hidden and dazzling.

Light-skinned black woman. One of those odd embodyings of doubtful language and unwavering race but the only words that meant anything to him were the ones she'd spoken and would speak.

She talked to God. Maybe Lianne had these conversations as well. He wasn't sure. Or long troubled monologues. Or shy thoughts. When she raised the subject or spoke the name he went blank. The matter was too abstract. Here, with a woman he barely knew, the matter seemed unavoidable, and other matters, other questions.

He heard the music change to something that had a buzz and drive, voices in Portuguese rapping, singing, whistling, with guitars and drums behind them, manic saxophones.

First she'd looked at him and then he'd watched her walk past the door and down the hall and now he knew that he was supposed to follow.

She stood by the window, clapping her hands to the music. It was a small bedroom, without a chair, and he sat on the floor and watched her.

"I've never been to Brazil," she said. "A place I think about sometimes."

"I'm talking to somebody. Very early in the talks. About a job involving Brazilian investors. I may need some Portuguese."

"We all need some Portuguese. We all need to go to Brazil. This is the disc that was in the player that you carried out of there."

He said, "Go ahead."

"What?"

"Dance."

"What?"

"Dance," he said. "You want to dance. I want to watch."

She stepped out of her shoes and began to dance, clapping hands softly to the beat and beginning to move toward him. She reached out a hand and he shook his head, smiling, and pushed back toward the wall. She was not practiced at this. This was not something she'd allow herself to do alone, he thought, or with someone else, or for someone else, not until now. She moved back across the room, seeming to lose herself in the music, eyes closed. She danced in slow motion for a time, no longer clapping, arms up and away from her body, nearly trancelike, and began to whirl in place, ever slower, facing him now, mouth open, eyes coming open.

Sitting there, watching, he began to crawl out of his clothes.

It happened to Rosellen S., an elemental fear out of deepest childhood. She could not remember where she lived. She stood alone on a corner near the elevated tracks, becoming desperate, separated from everything. She looked for a storefront, a street sign that might give her a clue. The world was receding, the simplest recognitions. She began to lose her sense of clarity, of distinctness. She was not lost so much as falling, growing fainter. Nothing lay around her but silence and distance. She wandered back the way she'd come, or thought she'd come, and went into a building and stood in the entranceway, listening. She followed the sound of voices and came to a room where a dozen people sat reading books, or one book, the Bible. When they saw her, they stopped reciting and waited. She tried to tell them what was wrong and one of them looked in her handbag and found numbers to call and finally got someone, a sister in Brooklyn, it turned out, listed as Billie, to come to East Harlem and take Rosellen home.

Lianne learned this from Dr. Apter the day after it happened. She'd seen the slow waning, over months. Rosellen still laughed at times, irony intact, a small woman of delicate features and chestnut skin. They approached what was impending, each of them, with a little space remaining, at this point, to stand and watch it happen.

Benny T. said he had trouble some mornings getting his pants on. Carmen said, "That's better than off." She said, "Long as you can get them off, sweetheart, you're the original sexy Benny." He laughed and stomped a little, battering himself on the head for effect, and said it wasn't really that kind of problem. He could not convince himself that the pants were on right. He put them on, took them off. He made certain the zipper was in front. He checked the length in the mirror, cuffs more or less on shoetops, except there were no cuffs. He remembered cuffs. These pants had cuffs yesterday so how come not today.

He said he knew how this sounded. It sounded peculiar to him too. He used this word, *peculiar*, avoiding more expressive terms. But when it was happening, he said, he could not get outside it. He was in a mind and body that were not his, looking at the fit. The pants did not seem to fit right. He took them off and put them on. He shook them out. He looked inside them. He began to think they were someone else's pants, in his house, draped over his chair.

They waited for Carmen to say something. Lianne waited for her to mention the fact that Benny wasn't married. Good thing you're not married, Benny, with some guy's pants on your chair. Your wife would have some explaining.

But Carmen said nothing this time.

Omar H. talked about the trip uptown. He was the only member of the group who lived out of the area, on the Lower East Side, and there was the subway, and the plastic card he had to swipe through the slot, swipe six times, change turnstiles, PLEASE SWIPE AGAIN, and the long ride uptown, and the time he landed somewhere on a raw corner in the Bronx, not knowing what had happened to the missing station stops.

Curtis B. could not find his wristwatch. When he found it, finally, in the medicine cabinet, he could not seem to attach it to his wrist. There it was, the watch. He said this gravely. There it was, in my right hand. But the right hand could not seem to find its way to the left wrist. There was a spatial void, or a visual gap, a rift in his field of vision, and it took him some time to make the connection, hand to wrist, pointed end of wristband into buckle. To Curtis this was a moral flaw, a sin of self-betrayal. Once at an earlier session he read a piece he'd written about an event fifty years earlier when he killed a man with a broken bottle in a bar fight, gouging the face and eyes and then severing the jugular. He looked up from the page when he spoke these words: *severing the jugular.*

He used the same deliberate tone, dark and fated, in his account of the lost watch.

Coming down the stairs she said something and it was only seconds after Keith did what he did that she made the connection. He kicked the door they were walking past. He stopped walking, eased back and kicked hard, striking the door with the bottom of his shoe.

Once she made the connection between what she'd said and what he did, the first thing she understood was that his anger was not directed at the music or at the woman who played the music. It was directed at her, for the remark, the complaint she'd made, the persistence of it, the vexing repetition.

The second thing she understood was that there was no anger. He was completely calm. He was playing out an emotion, hers, on her behalf, to her discredit. It was almost, she thought, a little Zenlike, a gesture to shock and stimulate one's meditations or reverse their direction.

No one came to the door. The music did not stop, a slowly circling figure of reeds and drums. They looked at each other and laughed, hard and loud, husband and wife, walking down the stairs and out the front door.

The poker games were at Keith's place, where the poker table was. There were six players, the regulars, Wednesday nights, the business writer, the adman, the mortgage broker and so on, men rolling their shoulders, hoisting their balls, ready to sit and play, game-faced, testing the forces that govern events.

In the beginning they played poker in a number of shapes and variations but over time they began to reduce the dealer's options. The banning of certain games started as a joke in the name of tradition and self-discipline but became effective over time, with arguments made against the shabbier aberrations. Finally the senior player, Dockery, pushing fifty, advocated straight poker only, the classical retro-format, five-card draw, five-card stud, seven-card stud, and with the shrinking of choice came the raising of stakes, which intensified the ceremony of check-writing for the long night's losers.

They played each hand in a glazed frenzy. All the action was somewhere behind the eyes, in naive expectation and calculated deceit. Each man tried to entrap the others and fix limits to his own false dreams, the bond trader, the lawyer, the other lawyer, and these games were the funneled essence, the clear and intimate extract of their daytime initiatives. The cards skimmed across the green baize surface of the round table. They used intuition and cold-war risk analysis. They used cunning and blind luck. They waited for the prescient moment, the time to make the bet based on the card they knew was coming. *Felt the queen and there it was.* They tossed in the chips and watched the eyes across the table. They regressed to preliterate folkways, petitioning the dead. There were elements of healthy challenge and outright mockery. There were elements of one's intent to shred the other's gauzy manhood.

Hovanis, dead now, decided at some point that they didn't need seven-card stud. The sheer number of cards and odds and options seemed excessive and the others laughed and made the rule, reducing the dealer's choice to five-card stud and five-card draw.

There was a corresponding elevation of stakes.

Then someone raised the question of food. This was a joke. There was food in casual platters on a counter in the kitchen. How disciplined can we be, Demetrius said, if we are taking time to leave the table and stuff our jaws with chemically treated breads, meats and cheeses. This was a joke they took seriously because leaving the table ought to be allowed only as a matter of severest bladder-racked urgency or the kind of running bad luck that requires a player to stand at the window looking out on the deep abiding tide of night.

So food was out. No food. They dealt the cards, they called or folded. Then they talked about liquor. They knew how stupid this was but they wondered, two or three of them, whether it might be advisable to narrow their intake to darkish liquors, to scotch, bourbon, brandy, the manlier tones and deeper and more intense distillations. No gin, no vodka, no wan liqueurs.

They enjoyed doing this, most of them. They liked creating a structure out of willful trivia. But not Terry Cheng, who played the sweetest game of poker, who played online at times for twenty hours straight. Terry Cheng said they were shallow people leading giddy lives.

Then someone made the point that five-card draw was even more permissive than seven-card stud and they wondered why they hadn't thought of this sooner, with the player's capacity to discard and draw as many as three cards, or to stand pat, or to fold if he sees fit, and they agreed to limit themselves to one game only, five-card stud, and the large sums they bet, the bright chips in stacks, the bluffs and counterbluffs, the elaborate curses and baleful stares, the dusky liquor in squat glasses, the cigar smoke collecting in stratiform patterns, the massive silent self-reproaches—these free-flowing energies and gestures were posed against the single counterforce, the fact of self-imposed restriction, all the more unyielding for being ordered from within.

No food. Food was out. No gin or vodka. No beer that was not dark. They issued a mandate against all beer that was not dark and against all dark beer that was not Beck's Dark. They did this because Keith told them a story he'd heard about a cemetery in Germany, in Cologne, where four good friends, card-players in a game that had lasted four or five decades, were buried in the configuration in which they'd been seated, invariably, at the card table, with two of the gravestones facing the other two, each player in his time-honored place.

They loved this story. It was a beautiful story about friendship and the transcendent effects of unremarkable habit. It made them reverent and thoughtful and one of the things they thought was that they had to cite Beck's Dark as the only dark because the beer was German and so were the cardplayers in the story.

Somebody wanted to ban sports talk. They banned sports talk, television talk, movie titles. Keith thought this was getting stupid. Rules are good, they replied, and the stupider the better. Rumsey the fartmeister, dead now, wanted to revoke all the prohibitions. Cigarettes were not prohibited. There was one cigarette smoker only and he was allowed to smoke all the cigarettes he wanted if he didn't mind appearing helpless and defective. Most of the others smoked cigars and felt expansive, grand in scale, sipping scotch or bourbon, finding synonyms for banned words such as *wet* and *dry*.

You are not serious people, said Terry Cheng. He said, Get serious or die.

The dealer skimmed the cards over the green baize, never failing to announce the name of the game, five-card stud, even though it was the only game they now played. The small dry irony of these announcements faded after a time and the words became a proud ritual, formal and indispensable, each dealer in turn, *five-card stud*, and they loved doing this, straight-faced, because where else would they encounter the kind of mellow tradition exemplified by the needless utterance of a few archaic words.

They played it safe and regretted it, took risks and lost, fell into states of lunar gloom. But there were always things to ban and rules to make.

Then one night it all fell apart. Somebody got hungry and demanded food. Somebody else pounded the table and said, *Food food.* This became a chant that filled the room. They rescinded the ban on food and demanded Polish vodka, some of them. They wanted pale spirits chilled in the freezer and served neat in short frosted tumblers. Other prohibitions fell, banned words were reinstated. They bet and raised, ate and drank, and from that point on resumed playing such games as high-low, acey-deucy, Chicago, Omaha, Texas hold 'em, anaconda and a couple of other deviant strains in poker's line of ancestry. But they missed, each dealer in turn, calling out the name of one game, five-card stud, to the exclusion of all other games, and they tried not to wonder what four other players would think of them, in this wallow of wild-man poker, tombstone to tombstone in Cologne.

At dinner they talked about a trip they might take to Utah during school break, to high valleys and clean winds, to breathable air, skiable slopes, and the kid sat with a biscuit in his fist, looking at the food on his plate.

"What do you think? Utah. Say it. Utah. A big leap forward from a sled in the park."

He looked at the dinner his father had prepared, wild salmon, gummy brown rice.

"He has nothing to say. He has passed beyond monosyllables," Keith said. "Remember when he spoke only in monosyllables. That lasted a while."

"Longer than I expected," she said.

"He has passed beyond that. He has gone to the next stage of his development."

"His spiritual development," she said.

"Total silence."

"Utter and unbreakable silence."

"Utah is the place for silent men. He'll live in the mountains."

"He'll live in a cave with insects and bats."

The kid slowly raised his head from the plate, looking at his father or into his father's clavicle, x-raying the slender bones beneath his father's shirt.

"How do you know the monosyllables were really a school thing? Maybe not," he said. "Because maybe it was Bill Lawton. Because maybe Bill Lawton talks in monosyllables."

Lianne sat back, shocked by this, by the name itself, hearing him say it.

"I thought Bill Lawton was a secret," Keith said. "Between the Siblings and you. And between you and me."

"You probably already told her. She probably already knows."

Keith looked at her and she tried to signal him that *no*, she hadn't said a thing about Bill Lawton. She gave him a clenched look, eyes narrowed, lips tight, trying to drill the look into his forebrain, like *no*.

"Nobody told anybody anything," Keith said. "Eat your fish."

The kid resumed looking at the plate.

"Because he does talk in monosyllables."

"All right. What does he say?"

There was no response. She tried to imagine what he was thinking. His father was back home now, living here, sleeping here, more or less as before, and he's thinking the man can't be trusted, can he? He sees the man as a figure that looms over the household, the man who went away once and came back and told the woman, who sleeps in the same bed as the man, all about Bill Lawton, so how can he be trusted to be here tomorrow.

If your child thinks you're guilty of something, right or wrong, then you're guilty. And it happens he was right.

"He says things that nobody knows but the Siblings and me."

"Tell us one of these things. In monosyllables," Keith said with an edge in his voice.

"No thank you."

"Is that what he says or is that what you say?"

"The whole point," he said, snapping the words clearly and defiantly, "is that he says things about the planes. We know they're coming because he says they are. But that's all I'm allowed to say. He says this time the towers will fall."

"The towers are down. You know this," she said softly.

"This time coming, he says, they'll really come down."

They talked to him. They tried to make gentle sense. She couldn't locate the menace she felt, listening to him. His repositioning of events frightened her in an unaccountable way. He was making something better than it really was, the towers still standing, but the time reversal, the darkness of the final thrust, how better becomes worse, these were the elements of a failed fairy tale, eerie enough but without coherence. It was the fairy tale children tell, not the one they listen to, devised by adults, and she changed the subject to Utah. Ski trails and true skies.

He looked into his plate. How different is a fish from a bird? One flies, the other swims. Maybe this is what he was thinking. He wouldn't eat a bird, would he, a goldfinch or a blue jay. Why should he eat a fish swimming wild in the ocean, caught with ten thousand other fish in a giant net on Channel 27?

One flies, the other swims.

This is what she felt in him, these stubborn thoughts, biscuit in his fist.

———

Keith walked through the park and came out on West 90th Street and it was strange, what he was seeing down by the community garden and coming toward him, a woman in the middle of the street, on horseback, wearing a yellow hard hat and carrying a riding crop, bobbing above the traffic, and it took him a long moment to understand that horse and rider had come out of a stable somewhere nearby and were headed toward the bridle path in the park.

It was something that belonged to another landscape, something inserted, a conjuring that resembled for the briefest second some half-seen image only half believed in the seeing, when the witness wonders what has happened to the meaning of things, to tree, street, stone, wind, simple words lost in the falling ash.

He used to come home late, looking shiny and a little crazy. This was the period, not long before the separation, when he took the simplest question as a form of hostile interrogation. He seemed to walk in the door waiting for her questions, prepared to stare right through her questions, but she had no interest in saying anything at all. She thought she knew by now. She understood by this time that it wasn't the drinking, or not that alone, and probably not some sport with a woman. He'd hide it better, she told herself. It was who he was, his native face, without the leveling element, the claims of social code.

Those nights, sometimes, he seemed on the verge of saying something, a sentence fragment, that was all, and it would end everything between them, all discourse, every form of stated arrangement, whatever drifts of love still lingered. He carried that glassy look in his eyes and a moist smile across his mouth, a dare to himself, boyish and horrible. But he did not put into words whatever it was that lay there, something so surely and recklessly cruel that it scared her, spoken or not. The look scared her, the body slant. He walked through the apartment, bent slightly to one side, a twisted guilt in his smile, ready to break up a table and burn it so he could take out his dick and piss on the flames.

They sat in a taxi going downtown and began to clutch each other, kissing and groping. She said, in urgent murmurs, *It's a movie, it's a movie*. At traffic lights people crossing the street stopped to watch, two or three, seeming briefly to float above the windows, and sometimes only one. The others just crossed, who didn't give a damn.

In the Indian restaurant the man at the podium said, We do not seat incomplete tables.

She asked him one night about the friends he'd lost. He spoke about them, Rumsey and Hovanis, and the one who was badly burned, whose name she'd forgotten. She'd met one of them, Rumsey, she thought, briefly, somewhere. He spoke only about their qualities, their personalities, or married or single, or children or not, and this was enough. She didn't want to hear more.

It was still there, more often than not, music on the stairs.

There was a job offer he'd probably accept, drafting contracts of sale on behalf of Brazilian investors who were engaged in real-estate transactions in New York. He made it sound like a ride on a hang glider, completely wind-assisted.

In the beginning she washed his clothes in a separate load. She had no idea why she did this. It was like he was dead.

She listened to what he said and let him know she was listening, mind and body, because listening is what would save them this time, keep them from falling into distortion and rancor.

The easy names were the ones she forgot. But this one wasn't easy and it was like the swaggering name of some football player from Alabama and that's how she remembered it, Demetrius, badly burned in the other tower, the south tower.

When she asked him about the briefcase in the closet, why it was there one day and gone the next, he said he'd actually returned it to the owner because it wasn't his and he didn't know why he'd taken it out of the building.

What was ordinary was not more ordinary than usual, or less.

It was the word *actually* that made her think about what he said concerning the briefcase, although in fact there was nothing to think about, even if this was the word he'd used so often, more or less superfluously, those earlier years, when he was lying to her, or baiting her, or even effecting some minor sleight.

This was the man who would not submit to her need for probing intimacy, overintimacy, the urge to ask, examine, delve, draw things out, trade secrets, tell everything. It was a need that had the body in it, hands, feet, genitals, scummy odors, clotted dirt, even if it was all talk or sleepy murmur. She wanted to absorb everything, childlike, the dust of stray sensation, whatever she could breathe in from other people's pores. She used to think she was other people. Other people have truer lives.

It's a movie, she kept saying, his hand in her pants, saying it, a moan in the shape of words, and at traffic lights people watched, a few, and the driver watched, lights or not, eyes gliding across the rearview mirror.

But then she might be wrong about what was ordinary. Maybe nothing was. Maybe there was a deep fold in the grain of things, the way things pass through the mind, the way time swings in the mind, which is the only place it meaningfully exists.

He listened to language tapes labeled South American Portuguese and practiced on the kid. He said, I speak only little Portuguese, saying this in English, with a Latin accent, and Justin tried not to smile.

She read newspaper profiles of the dead, every one that was printed. Not to read them, every one, was an offense, a violation of responsibility and trust. But she also read them because she had to, out of some need she did not try to interpret.

After the first time they made love he was in the bathroom, at first light, and she got up to dress for her morning run but then pressed herself naked to the full-length mirror, face turned, hands raised to roughly head level. She pressed her body to the glass, eyes shut, and stayed for a long moment, nearly collapsed against the cool surface, abandoning herself to it. Then she put on her shorts and top and was lacing her shoes when he came out of the bathroom, clean-shaven, and saw the fogged marks of her face, hands, breasts and thighs stamped on the mirror.

He sat alongside the table, left forearm placed along the near edge, hand dangling from the adjoining edge. He worked on the hand shapes, the bend of the wrist toward the floor, the bend of the wrist toward the ceiling. He used the uninvolved hand to apply pressure to the involved hand.

The wrist was fine, the wrist was normal. He'd thrown away the splint and stopped using the ice. But he sat alongside the table, two or three times a day now, curling the left hand into a gentle fist, forearm flat on the table, thumb raised in certain setups. He did not need the instruction sheet. It was automatic, the wrist extensions, the ulnar deviations, hand raised, forearm flat. He counted the seconds, he counted the repetitions.

———————

There were the mysteries of word and glance but also this, that every time they saw each other there was something tentative at first, a little stilted.

"I see them on the street now and then."

"Stopped me cold for a moment. A horse," he said.

"Man on a horse. Woman on a horse. Not something I would think of doing myself," Florence said. "Give me all your money. Wouldn't matter. I'm not getting on a horse."

There was a shyness for a time and then something that eased the mood, a look or a wisecrack or the way she begins to hum, in a parody of social desperation, eyes darting about the room. But the faint discomfort of those early moments, the sense of ill-matched people was not completely dispelled.

"Sometimes six or seven horses single file, going up the street. The riders looking straight ahead," she said, "like the natives might take offense."

"I'll tell you what surprises me."

"Is it my eyes? Is it my lips?"

"It's your cat," he said.

"I don't have a cat."

"That's what surprises me."

"You think I'm a cat person."

"I see you with a cat, definitely. There ought to be a cat slipping along the walls."

He was in the armchair this time and she'd placed a kitchen chair alongside and sat facing him, a hand on his forearm.

"Tell me you're not taking the job."

"Have to do it."

"What happens to our time together?"

"We'll work it out."

"I want to blame you for this. But my turn is coming. Looks like the whole company is moving across the river. Permanently. We'll have a nice view of lower Manhattan. What's left of it."

"And you'll find a place to live somewhere nearby."

She looked at him.

"Can you mean that? I don't believe you said that. Do you think I'd put that much space between us?"

"Bridge or tunnel doesn't matter. It's hell on earth, that commute."

"I don't care. Do you think I care? They'll resume train service. If they don't, I'll drive."

"Okay."

"It's only Jersey."

"Okay," he said.

He thought she might cry. He thought this kind of conversation was for other people. People have these conversations all the time, he thought, in rooms like this one, sitting, looking.

Then she said, "You saved my life. Don't you know that?"

He sat back, looking at her.

"I saved your briefcase."

And waited for her to laugh.

"I can't explain it but no, you saved my life. After what happened, so many gone, friends gone, people I worked with, I was nearly gone, nearly dead, in another way. I couldn't see people, talk to people, go from here to there without forcing myself up off the chair. Then you walked in the door. I kept calling the number of a friend, missing, she's one of the photographs on the walls and windows everywhere, Davia, officially missing, I can barely say her name, in the middle of the night, dial the number, let it ring. I was afraid, in the daytime, other people would be there to pick up the phone, somebody who knew something I didn't want to hear. Then you walked in the door. You ask yourself why you took the briefcase out of the building. That's why. So you could bring it here. So we could get to know each other. That's why you took it and that's why you brought it here, to keep me alive."

He didn't believe this but he believed her. She felt it and meant it.

"You ask yourself what the story is that goes with the brief-case. I'm the story," she said.

7

The two dark objects, the white bottle, the huddled boxes. Lianne turned away from the painting and saw the room itself as a still life, briefly. Then the human figures appear, Mother and Lover, with Nina still in the armchair, thinking remotely of something, and Martin hunched on the sofa now, facing her.

Finally her mother said, "Architecture, yes, maybe, but coming out of another time entirely, another century. Office towers, no. These shapes are not translatable to modern towers, twin towers. It's work that rejects that kind of extension or projection. It takes you inward, down and in. That's what I see there, half buried, something deeper than things or shapes of things."

Lianne knew, in a pinprick of light, what her mother was going to say.

She said, "It's all about mortality, isn't it?"

"Being human," Lianne said.

"Being human, being mortal. I think these pictures are what I'll look at when I've stopped looking at everything else. I'll look at bottles and jars. I'll sit here looking."

"You'll need to move the chair a little closer."

"I'll push the chair up to the wall. I'll call the maintenance man and have him push the chair for me. I'll be too frail to do it myself. I'll look and I'll muse. Or I'll just look. After a while I won't need the paintings to look at. The paintings will be excess. I'll look at the wall."

Lianne crossed to the sofa, where she gave Martin a light poke in the arm.

"What about your walls? What's on your walls?"

"My walls are bare. Home and office. I keep bare walls," he said.

"Not completely," Nina said.

"All right, not completely."

She was looking at him.

"You tell us to forget God."

The argument had been here all this time, in the air and on the skin, but the shift in tone was abrupt.

"You tell us this is history."

Nina looked at him, she stared hard at Martin, her voice marked by accusation.

"But we can't forget God. They invoke God constantly. This is their oldest source, their oldest word. Yes, there's something else but it's not history or economics. It's what men feel. It's the thing that happens among men, the blood that happens when an idea begins to travel, whatever's behind it, whatever blind force or blunt force or violent need. How convenient it is to find a system of belief that justifies these feelings and these killings."

"But the system doesn't justify this. Islam renounces this," he said.

"If you call it God, then it's God. God is whatever God allows."

"Don't you realize how bizarre that is? Don't you see what you're denying? You're denying all human grievance against others, every force of history that places people in conflict."

"We're talking about these people, here and now. It's a mis-

112

placed grievance. It's a viral infection. A virus reproduces itself outside history."

He sat hunched and peering, leaning toward her now.

"First they kill you, then you try to understand them. Maybe, eventually, you'll learn their names. But they have to kill you first."

It went on for a time and Lianne listened, disturbed by the fervor in their voices. Martin sat wrapped in argument, one hand gripping the other, and he spoke about lost lands, failed states, foreign intervention, money, empire, oil, the narcissistic heart of the West, and she wondered how he did the work he did, made the living he made, moving art, taking profit. Then there were the bare walls. She wondered about that.

Nina said, "I'm going to smoke a cigarette now."

This eased the tension in the room, the way she said it, gravely, an announcement and an event suitably consequential, measured to the level of discussion. Martin laughed, coming out of his tight crouch and heading to the kitchen for another beer.

"Where's my grandson? He's doing my portrait in crayon."

"You had a cigarette twenty minutes ago."

"I'm sitting for my portrait. I need to unwind."

"He gets out of school in two hours. Keith is going to pick him up."

"Justin and I. We need to talk about skin color, flesh tones."

"He likes white."

"He's thinking very white. Like paper."

"He uses bright colors for the eyes, the hair, maybe the mouth. Where we see flesh, he sees white."

"He's thinking paper, not flesh. The work is a fact in itself. The subject of the portrait is the paper."

Martin walked in licking foam from the rim of the glass.

"Does he have a white crayon?"

"He doesn't need a white crayon. He has white paper," she said.

He stopped to look at the vintage passport photos on the south wall, stained with age, and Nina watched him.

"So beautiful and so dignified," she said, "those people and those photographs. I've just renewed my passport. Ten years come and gone, like a sip of tea. I've never cared much about how I look in photographs. Not the way some people do. But this photograph scares me."

"Where are you going?" Lianne said.

"I don't have to go anywhere to own a passport."

Martin came around to her chair and stood behind it, leaning over to speak softly.

"You should go somewhere. An extended trip, when we get back from Connecticut. No one is traveling now. You should think about this."

"Not a good idea."

"Far away," he said.

"Far away."

"Cambodia. Before the jungle overtakes what remains. I'll go with you if you like."

Her mother smoked a cigarette like a woman in the 1940s, in a gangster film, all nervous urgency, in black and white.

"I look at the face in the passport photo. Who is that woman?"

"I lift my head from the washbasin," Martin said.

"Who is that man? You think you see yourself in the mirror. But that's not you. That's not what you look like. That's not the literal face, if there is such a thing, ever. That's the composite face. That's the face in transition."

"Don't tell me this."

"What you see is not what we see. What you see is distracted by memory, by being who you are, all this time, for all these years."

"I don't want to hear this," he said.

"What we see is the living truth. The mirror softens the effect by submerging the actual face. Your face is your life. But your face is also submerged in your life. That's why you don't see it. Only other people see it. And the camera of course."

He smiled into his glass. Nina put out her cigarette, barely smoked, waving away a trail of smeary mist.

"Then there's the beard," Lianne said.

"The beard helps bury the face."

"It's not much of a beard."

"But that's the art of it," Nina said.

"The art of looking unkempt."

"Unkempt but deeply sensitive."

"This is American kidding. Am I right?" he said.

"The beard's a nice device."

"He speaks to it," Nina said. "Every morning, in the mirror."

"What does he say?"

"He speaks in German. The beard is German."

"I am flattered, right?" he said. "To be the subject of such kidding."

"The nose is Austro-Hungarian."

He leaned toward Nina, still standing behind her, touching the back of his hand to her face. Then he took the empty glass to the kitchen and the two women sat quietly for a moment. Lianne wanted to go home and sleep. Her mother wanted to sleep, she wanted to sleep. She wanted to go home and talk to Keith for a while and then fall into bed, fall asleep. Talk to Keith or not talk at all. But she wanted him to be there when she got home.

Martin spoke from the far end of the room, surprising them.

"They want their place in the world, their own global union, not ours. It's an old dead war, you say. But it's everywhere and it's rational."

"Fooled me."

"Don't be fooled. Don't think people will die only for God," he said.

His cell phone buzzed and he altered his stance, turning toward the wall and seeming to speak into his chest. These fragments of conversation, which Lianne had heard before, from a distance, included English, French and German phrases, depending on the caller, and sometimes a small jeweled syllable such as *Braque* or *Johns*.

He finished quickly and put the phone away.

"Travel, yes, it's a thing you ought to consider," he said. "Get your knee back to normal and we'll go, quite seriously."

"Far away."

"Far away."

"Ruins," she said.

"Ruins."

"We have our own ruins. But I don't think I want to see them."

He moved along the wall toward the door.

"But that's why you built the towers, isn't it? Weren't the towers built as fantasies of wealth and power that would one day become fantasies of destruction? You build a thing like that so you can see it come down. The provocation is obvious. What other reason would there be to go so high and then to double it, do it twice? It's a fantasy, so why not do it twice? You are saying, Here it is, bring it down."

Then he opened the door and was gone.

———

He watched poker on television, pained faces in a casino complex in the desert. He watched without interest. It wasn't poker, it was television. Justin came in and watched with him and he outlined the game to the kid, in snatches, as the players paused and raised and the strategies unfolded. Then Lianne came in and sat on the floor, watching her son. He was seated at a radical slant, barely in contact with the chair and staring helplessly into the glow, a victim of alien abduction.

She looked at the screen, faces in close-up. The game itself faded into anesthesia, the tedium of a hundred thousand dollars won or lost on the flip of a card. It meant nothing. It was outside her interest or sympathy. But the players were interesting. She watched the players, they drew her in, deadpan, drowsy, slouched, men in misfortune, she thought, making a leap to Kierkegaard, somehow, and recalling the long nights she'd spent with her head in a text. She watched the screen and imagined a northern bleakness, faces misplaced in the desert. Wasn't there a soul struggle, a sense of continuing dilemma, even in the winner's little blink of winning?

She said nothing about this to Keith, who would have turned half toward her, gazing into space in mock contemplation, mouth open, eyelids slowly closing and head sinking finally to his chest.

He was thinking of being here, Keith was, and not thinking of it but only feeling it, alive to it. He saw her face reflected in a corner of the screen. He was watching the cardplayers and noting the details of move and countermove but also watching her and feeling this, the sense of being here with them. He had a single-malt scotch in his fist. He heard a car alarm sounding down the street. He reached over and knocked on Justin's head, knock knock, to alert him to a revelation in the making as the camera located the hole cards of a player who didn't know he was dead.

117

"He's dead," he told his son, and the kid sat without comment in his makeshift diagonal, half in the chair, half on the floor, semi-mesmerized.

She loved Kierkegaard in his antiqueness, in the glaring drama of the translation she owned, an old anthology of brittle pages with ruled underlinings in red ink, passed down by someone in her mother's family. This is what she read and re-read into deep night in her dorm room, a drifting mass of papers, clothing, books and tennis gear that she liked to think of as the objective correlative of an overflowing mind. What *is* an objective correlative? What *is* cognitive dissonance? She used to know the answers to everything then, it seemed to her now, and she used to love Kierkegaard right down to the spelling of his name. The hard Scandian *k*'s and lovely doubled *a*. Her mother sent books all the time, great dense demanding fiction, airtight and relentless, but it defeated her eager need for self-recognition, something closer to mind and heart. She read her Kierkegaard with a feverish expectancy, straight into the Protestant badlands of sickness unto death. Her roommate wrote punk lyrics for an imaginary band called Piss in My Mouth and Lianne envied her creative desperation. Kierkegaard gave her a danger, a sense of spiritual brink. *The whole of existence frightens me,* he wrote. She saw herself in this sentence. He made her feel that her thrust into the world was not the slender melodrama she sometimes thought it was.

She watched the faces of the cardplayers, then caught her husband's eye, onscreen, in reflection, watching her, and she smiled. There was the amber drink in his hand. There was the car alarm sounding somewhere along the street, a reassuring feature of familiar things, safe night settling in. She reached over and snatched the kid from his roost. Before he went off to bed, Keith asked him if he wanted a set of poker chips and a deck of cards.

The answer was maybe, which meant yes.

Finally she had to do it and then she did, knocking on the door, hard, and waiting for Elena to open even as voices trembled within, women in soft chorus, singing in Arabic.

Elena had a dog named Marko. Lianne remembered this the instant she hit the door. Marko, she thought, with a *k*, whatever that might signify.

She hit the door again, this time with the flat of her hand, and then the woman stood there, in tailored jeans and a sequined T-shirt.

"The music. All the time, day and night. And loud."

Elena stared into her, radiating a lifetime of alertness to insult.

"Don't you know this? We hear it on the stairs, we hear it in our apartments. All the time, day and fucking night."

"What is it? Music, that's all. I like it. It's beautiful. It gives me peace. I like it, I play it."

"Why now? This particular time?"

"Now, later, what's the difference? It's music."

"But why now and why so loud?"

"Nobody ever complained. This is the first time I'm hearing loud. It's not so loud."

"It's loud."

"It's music. You want to take it personally, what can I tell you?"

Marko came to the door, a hundred and thirty pounds, black, with deep fur and webbed feet.

"Of course it's personal. Anybody would take it personally. Under these circumstances. There are circumstances. You acknowledge this, don't you?"

"There are no circumstances. It's music," she said. "It gives me peace."

"But why now?"

"The music has nothing to do with now or then or any other time. And nobody ever said loud."

"It's fucking loud."

"You must be ultrasensitive, which I would never think from hearing the language you use."

"The whole city is ultrasensitive right now. Where have you been hiding?"

Every time she saw the dog out in the street, half a block away, with Elena carrying a plastic baggie to harvest his shit, she thought Marko with a *k*.

"It's music. I like it, I play it. You think it's so loud, walk faster on your way out the door."

Lianne put her hand in the woman's face.

"It gives you peace," she said.

She twisted her open hand in Elena's face, under the left eye, and pushed her back into the entranceway.

"It gives you peace," she said.

Marko backed into the apartment, barking. Lianne mashed the hand into the eye and the woman took a swing at her, a blind right that caught the edge of the door. Lianne knew she was going crazy even as she turned and walked out, slamming the door behind her and hearing the dog bark over the sound of a solo lute from Turkey or Egypt or Kurdistan.

Rumsey sat in a cubicle not far from the north facade, a hockey stick propped in a corner. He and Keith played in pickup games at Chelsea Piers at two in the morning. In warmer months they wandered the streets and plazas at lunchtime, in the rippling shadows of the towers, looking at women, talking about women, telling stories, taking comfort.

Keith separated, living nearby for convenience, eating for convenience, checking the running time of rented movies before he took them out of the store. Rumsey single, in an affair with a married woman, recently arrived from Malaysia, who sold T-shirts and postcards on Canal Street.

Rumsey had compulsions. He admitted this to his friend. He admitted everything, concealed nothing. He counted parked cars in the street, windows in a building a block away. He counted the steps he took, here to there. He memorized things that crossed his consciousness, streams of information, more or less unwillingly. He could recite the personal data of a couple of dozen friends and acquaintances, addresses, phone numbers, birthdays. Months after the file of a random client crossed his desk, he could tell you the man's mother's maiden name.

This was not cute stuff. There was an open pathos in the man. At the hockey rink, in poker games, they shared a recognition, he and Keith, an intuitive sense of the other's methodology as teammate or opponent. He was ordinary in many ways, Rumsey, a broad and squarish body, an even temperament, but he took his ordinariness to the deep end at times. He was forty-one, in a suit and tie, walking through promenades, in waves of beating heat, looking for women in open-toed sandals.

All right. He was compelled to count things including the digits that constitute the foreparts of a woman's foot. He admitted this. Keith did not laugh. He tried to see it as routine human business, unfathomable, something people do, all of us, in one form or another, in the off moments of living the lives others think we are living. He did not laugh, then he did. But he understood that the fixation was not directed toward sexual ends. It was the counting that mattered, even if the outcome was established in advance. Toes on one foot, toes on the other. Always totaling ten.

Keith tall, five or six inches taller than his friend. He saw male pattern baldness develop in Rumsey, seemingly week by week, on their noontime walks, or Rumsey slumped in his cubicle, or holding a sandwich with both hands, head lowered to eat. He carried bottled water everywhere. He memorized the numbers on license plates even as he drove.

Keith seeing a woman with two kids, goddamn. She lived in Far fucking Rockaway.

Women on benches or steps, reading or doing crosswords, sunning themselves, heads thrown back, or scooping yogurt with blue spoons, sandaled women, some of them, toes exposed.

Rumsey eyes down, following the puck across the ice, body crashing the boards, free of aberrant need for a couple of happy shattering hours.

Keith running in place, on a treadmill at the gym, voices in his head, mostly his own, even when he wore a headset, listening to books on tape, science or history.

The counting always led to ten. This was not a discouragement or impediment. Ten is the beauty of it. Ten is probably why I do it. To get that sameness, Rumsey said. Something holds, something stays in place.

Rumsey's girlfriend wanted him to invest in the business she ran with three relatives including her husband. They wanted to add stock, add running shoes and personal electronics.

The toes meant nothing if they were not defined by sandals. Barefoot women on the beach were not about their feet.

He compiled bonus miles on his credit cards and flew to cities chosen strictly for their distance from New York, just to use the miles. It satisfied some principle of emotional credit.

There were men in open-toed sandals, here and there, in the streets and parks, but Rumsey did not count their toes. So maybe it wasn't just the counting that mattered. One had to factor in the women. He admitted this. He admitted everything.

The persistence of the man's needs had a kind of crippled appeal. It opened Keith to dimmer things, at odder angles, to something crouched and uncorrectable in people but also capable of stirring a warm feeling in him, a rare tinge of affinity.

Baldness in Rumsey, as it progressed, was a gentle melancholy, the pensive regret of a failed boy.

They fought once, briefly, on the ice, teammates, by mistake, in a mass brawl, and Keith thought it was funny but Rumsey was angry, a little shrill with accusation, claiming that Keith threw a few additional punches after he realized who it was he was hitting, which wasn't true, Keith said, but thought it might be, because once the thing starts, what recourse is there?

They walked toward the towers now, amid the sweep and crisscross of masses of people.

All right. But what if the digits don't always total ten? You're riding the subway, say, and you're sitting eyes down, Keith said, and you're absentmindedly scanning the aisle, and you see a pair of sandals, and you count and count again, and there are nine digits, or eleven.

Rumsey took this question with him up to his cubicle in the sky, where he went back to work on less arresting matters, on money and property, contracts and titles.

One day later he said, I would ask her to marry me.

And later still, Because I would understand that I was cured, like Lourdes, and could stop counting now.

Keith watched her across the table.

"When did it happen?"

"About an hour ago."

"That dog," he said.

"I know. It was a crazy thing to do."

123

"What happens now? You'll see her in the hall."

"I don't apologize. That's what happens."

He sat and nodded, watching her.

"Hate to say it but when I came up the stairs just now."

"You don't have to say it."

"The music was playing," he said.

"I guess that means she wins."

"No louder, no softer."

"She wins."

He said, "Maybe she's dead. Lying there."

"Dead or alive, she wins."

"That dog."

"I know. It was totally crazy. I could hear myself speaking. My voice was like it was coming from somebody else."

"I've seen that animal. The kid fears that animal. Won't say it but does."

"What is it?"

"A Newfoundland."

"The whole province," she said.

"You're lucky."

"Lucky and crazy. Marko."

He said, "Forget the music."

"He spells his name with a *k*."

"So do I. Forget the music," he said. "It's not a message or a lesson."

"But it's still playing."

"It's still playing because she's dead. Lying there. Being sniffed by big dog."

"I need to get more sleep. That's what I need," she said.

"Big dog sniffing dead woman's crotch."

"I wake up at some point every night. Mind running non-stop. Can't stop it."

"Forget the music."

"Thoughts I can't identify, thoughts I can't claim as mine."

He kept watching her.

"Take something. Your mother knows about this. This is how people sleep."

"I have a history with the things people take. They make me crazier. They make me stupid, make me forget."

"Talk to your mother. She knows about this."

"Can't stop it, can't go back to sleep. Takes forever. Then it's morning," she said.

The truth was mapped in slow and certain decline. Each member of the group lived in this knowledge. Lianne found it hardest to accept in the case of Carmen G. She appeared to be two women simultaneously, the one sitting here, less combative over time, less clearly defined, speech beginning to drag, and the younger and slimmer and wildly attractive one, as Lianne imagines her, a spirited woman in her reckless prime, funny and blunt, spinning on a dance floor.

Lianne herself, bearing her father's mark, the potential toll of plaque and twisted filaments, had to look at this woman and see the crime of it, the loss of memory, personality and identity, the lapse into eventual protein stupor. There was the page she wrote and then read aloud, meant to be an account of her day, yesterday. This was not the piece they'd all agreed to write. This was Carmen's piece.

I wake up thinking where's everybody. I'm alone because that's who I am. I'm thinking where's the rest of them, wide awake, don't want to get up. It's like I need my documents to get out of bed. Prueba de ingreso. Prueba de dirección. Tarjeta de seguro social. Picture ID. My father who told jokes he didn't care

clean or dirty the kids have to learn these things. I had two hus-
bands they were different except for their hands. I still look at a
man's hands. Because somebody said it's a question of which
brain is working today because everybody has two brains. Why is
it the hardest thing in the world, get out of bed. I have a plant
that needs water all the time. I never thought a plant could be
work.

Benny said, "But where's your day? You said this is your
day."

"This is the first like ten seconds. This is still in bed. Next
time we're here maybe I finish getting out of bed. Next time after
that I wash my hands. That's day three. Day four, my face."

Benny said, "We live that long? By the time you take a pee
we all be fatal."

Then it was her turn. They'd been asking and then urging.
They'd all written something, said something about the planes.
It was Omar H. who brought it up again, in his earnest way, right
arm raised.

"Where were you when it happened?"

For nearly two years now, ever since the storyline sessions
began, with her marriage receding into the night sky, she'd listened to these men and women speak about their lives in funny,
stinging, straightforward and moving ways, binding the trust
among them.

She owed them a story, didn't she?

There was Keith in the doorway. Always that, had to be
that, the desperate sight of him, alive, her husband. She tried to
follow the sequence of events, seeing him as she spoke, a figure
floating in reflected light, Keith in pieces, in small strokes. The
words came fast. She recalled things she didn't know she'd
absorbed, the fragment of spangled glass on the lid of his eye, as
if sewn there, and how they'd walked to the hospital, nine or ten

blocks, in near deserted streets, in halting steps and deepest silence, and the young man who assisted, a deliveryman, a kid, helping support Keith with one hand and holding a pizza carton with the other, and she nearly asked him how someone could phone in an order for takeout if the phones were not working, a tall Latino kid but maybe not, holding the carton by the bottom, balanced on the palm of his hand and out away from his body.

She wanted to stay focused, one thing following sensibly upon another. There were moments when she wasn't talking so much as fading into time, dropping back into some funneled stretch of recent past. They sat dead still, watching her. People, lately, watched her. She seemingly needed watching. They were depending on her to make sense. They were waiting for words from her side of the line, where what is solid does not melt.

She told them about her son. When he was nearby, within sight or touch, in himself, in motion, the fear eased off. Other times she could not think of him without being afraid. This was Justin disembodied, the child of her devising.

Unattended packages, she said, or the menace of lunch in a paper bag, or the subway at rush hour, down there, in sealed boxes.

She could not look at him sleep. He became a child in some jutting future. What do children know? They know who they are, she said, in ways we can't know and they can't tell us. There are moments frozen in the run of routine hours. She could not look at him sleep without thinking of what was yet to come. It was part of his stillness, figures in a silent distance, fixed in windows.

Please report any suspicious behavior or unattended packages. That was the wording, wasn't it?

She almost told them about the briefcase, the fact of its appearance and disappearance and what it meant if anything.

Wanted to tell them but did not. Tell them everything, say everything. She needed them to listen.

Keith used to want more of the world than there was time and means to acquire. He didn't want this anymore, whatever it was he'd wanted, in real terms, real things, because he'd never truly known.

Now he wondered whether he was born to be old, meant to be old and alone, content in lonely old age, and whether all the rest of it, all the glares and rants he had bounced off these walls, were simply meant to get him to that point.

This was his father seeping through, sitting home in western Pennsylvania, reading the morning paper, taking the walk in the afternoon, a man braided into sweet routine, a widower, eating the evening meal, unconfused, alive in his true skin.

There was a second level to the high-low games. Terry Cheng was the player who divided the chips, half to each winner, high and low. He'd do it in seconds, stacking chips of different colors and varying denominations in two columns or two sets of columns, depending on the size of the pot. He did not want columns so high they might topple. He did not want columns that looked alike. The idea was to arrive at two allotments of equal monetary value but never of evenly distributed colors, or anything close to that. He'd stack six blue chips, four gold, three red and five white and then match this, with steel-trap speed, fingers flying, hands sometimes crossing, with sixteen white, four blue, two gold and thirteen red, building his columns and then folding his arms and looking into secret space, leaving each winner to rake in his chips, in unspoken respect and semi-awe.

No one doubted his skills of hand-eye-mind. No one tried to count along with Terry Cheng and no one ever harbored the thought, even in the brooding depths of the night, that Terry Cheng might be wrong in his high-low determinations, just this once.

Keith talked to him on the telephone, twice, briefly, after the planes. Then they stopped calling each other. There was nothing left, it seemed, to say about the others in the game, lost and injured, and there was no general subject they might comfortably summon. Poker was the one code they shared and that was over now.

Her schoolmates called her Gawk for a time. Then it was Scrawn. This was not necessarily a case of hateful naming, coming mostly from friends and often with her connivance. She liked to pose in parody of a model on a runway, only all elbows, knees and wired teeth. When she began to grow out of her angularity, there were the times her father rolled into town, sunburnt Jack, shooting out his arms when he saw her, a beautifully burgeoning creature he loved in muscle and blood, until he went away again. But she remembered these times, his stance and smile, the half crouch, the set of his jaw. He'd shoot out his arms and she'd fall shyly into the enclosing fold. This was ever Jack, hugging and shaking her, looking so deeply into her eyes it seemed at times he was trying to place her in proper context.

She was darkish, unlike him, with large eyes and wide mouth and with an eagerness that could be startling to others, a readiness to encounter an occasion or idea. Her mother was the template for this.

Her father used to say of her mother, "She's a sexy woman except for her skinny ass."

Lianne was thrilled by the chummy vulgarity, the invitation to share the man's special perspective, his openness of reference and slant rhyme.

It was Jack's perspective on architecture that had drawn Nina. They met on a small island in the northeast Aegean where Jack had designed a cluster of white stucco dwellings for an artists' retreat. Set above a cove, the grouping, from offshore, was a piece of pure geometry gone slightly askew—Euclidean rigor in quantum space, Nina would write.

Here on a hard cot, on a second visit, was where Lianne was conceived. Jack told her this when she was twelve years old and would not refer to it again until he called from New Hampshire, ten years later, saying the same things in the same words, the sea breeze, the hard cot, the music floating up from the waterfront, sort of Greek-Oriental. This was some minutes or hours, this phone call, before he gazed into the muzzle blast.

They were watching TV without the sound.

"My father shot himself so I would never have to face the day when he failed to know who I was."

"You believe this."

"Yes."

"Then I believe it too," he said.

"The fact that he would one day fail to recognize me."

"I believe it," he said.

"That's absolutely why he did it."

She was slightly drunk after an extra glass of wine. They were watching a late-night newscast and he thought of hitting the sound button when the commercials ended but then did not and they watched in silence as a correspondent in a desolate landscape, Afghanistan or Pakistan, pointed over his shoulder to mountains in the distance.

"We need to get him a book on birds."

"Justin," he said.

"They're studying birds. Each kid gets to choose a bird and that's the bird he or she studies. That's his or her feathered vertebrate. His for boys. Hers for girls."

There was stock footage on the screen of fighter planes lifting off the deck of a carrier. He waited for her to ask him to hit the sound button.

"He's talking about a kestrel. What the hell's a kestrel?" she said.

"It's a small falcon. We saw them perched on power lines, mile after mile, when we were somewhere out west, back in the other life."

"The other life," she said, and laughed, and pushed up off the chair, headed for the bathroom.

"Come out wearing something," he said, "so I can watch you take it off."

Florence Givens stood looking at the mattresses, forty or fifty of them, arranged in rows at one end of the ninth floor. People tested the bedding, women mostly, bouncing lightly in seated positions or lying supine, checking for firmness or plushness. It took her a moment to realize that Keith was standing at her side, watching with her.

"Right on time," she said.

"You're the one who's on time. I've been here for hours," he said, "riding the escalators."

They walked along the aisle and she stopped several times to check labels and prices and to press into the bedding with the heel of her hand.

He said, "Go on, lie down."

"I don't think I want to do that."

"How else will you know if this is the mattress you want? Look around. They're all doing it."

"I'll lie down if you'll lie down."

"I don't need a mattress," he said. "You need a mattress."

She wandered along the aisle. He stood and watched and there were ten or eleven women lying on beds, bouncing on beds, and a man and a woman bouncing and rolling, middle-aged and purposeful, trying to determine if one person's tossing would disturb the other's sleep.

There were tentative women, bouncing once or twice, feet protruding from the end of the bed, and there were the others, women who'd shed their coats and shoes, falling backwards to the mattress, the Posturepedic or the Beautyrest, and bouncing with abandon, first one side of the bed, then the other, and he thought this was a remarkable thing to come upon, the mattress department at Macy's, and he looked across the aisle and they were bouncing there as well, another eight or nine women, one man, one child, testing for comfort and sculptural soundness, for back support and foam sensation.

Florence was over there now, seated at the end of a bed, and she smiled at him and fell back. She bounced up, fell back, making a little game of her shyness in the midst of public intimacy. Two men stood not far from Keith and one of them said something to the other. It was a remark about Florence. He didn't know what the man had said but it didn't matter. It was clear from their stance and their vantage that Florence was the subject.

Keith stood ten paces away from them.

He said, "Hey fuckhead."

The idea was that they'd meet here, have a quick lunch nearby and go their separate ways. He had to pick up the kid at school, she had a doctor's appointment. It was a tryst without whisper or touch, set among strangers falling down.

He said it again, louder this time, and waited for the word to register. It was interesting, how the space between them changed. They were looking at him now. The man who'd made the remark was heavyset, in a shiny down jacket that resembled bubblewrap. People drifted along the aisle, in blurry colors. Both men were looking at him. The space was hot and charged and the one in bubblewrap stood brooding on the matter. Women were bouncing on the beds but Florence had seen and heard and she was seated at the edge of the mattress, watching.

The man was listening to his companion but did not move. Keith was happy to stand and watch and then he wasn't. He walked over there and punched the man. He walked over, stopped, set himself and threw a short right. He hit the man up near the cheekbone, one blow only, and then he stepped back and waited. He was angry now. The contact set him off and he wanted to keep going. He held his hands apart, palms up, like here I am, let's go. Because if anyone said a harsh word to Florence, or raised a hand to Florence, or insulted her in any way, Keith was ready to kill him.

The man, who'd lurched against his companion, turned now and charged, head down, arms bowed out, like a guy on a motorcycle, and the bouncing stopped all along the rows of beds.

Keith caught him with another right, to the eye this time, and the man lifted him off the floor, an inch or two, and Keith threw some kidney punches that were mostly lost in bubblewrap. There were men everywhere now, salesmen, security guards jogging down the aisle, a workman who'd been pushing a handcart. It was odd, in the general confusion after they'd been separated, how Keith felt a hand on his arm, just above the elbow, and understood at once that it was Florence.

Every time she saw a videotape of the planes she moved a finger toward the power button on the remote. Then she kept on watching. The second plane coming out of that ice blue sky, this was the footage that entered the body, that seemed to run beneath her skin, the fleeting sprint that carried lives and histories, theirs and hers, everyone's, into some other distance, out beyond the towers.

The skies she retained in memory were dramas of cloud and sea storm, or the electric sheen before summer thunder in the city, always belonging to the energies of sheer weather, of what was out there, air masses, water vapor, westerlies. This was different, a clear sky that carried human terror in those streaking aircraft, first one, then the other, the force of men's intent. He watched with her. Every helpless desperation set against the sky, human voices crying to God and how awful to imagine this, God's name on the tongues of killers and victims both, first one plane and then the other, the one that was nearly cartoon human, with flashing eyes and teeth, the second plane, the south tower.

He watched with her one time only. She knew she'd never felt so close to someone, watching the planes cross the sky. Standing by the wall he reached toward the chair and took her hand. She bit her lip and watched. They would all be dead, passengers and crew, and thousands in the towers dead, and she felt it in her body, a deep pause, and thought there he is, unbelievably, in one of those towers, and now his hand on hers, in pale light, as though to console her for his dying.

He said, "It still looks like an accident, the first one. Even from this distance, way outside the thing, how many days later, I'm standing here thinking it's an accident."

"Because it has to be."

"It has to be," he said.

"The way the camera sort of shows surprise."

"But only the first one."

"Only the first," she said.

"The second plane, by the time the second plane appears," he said, "we're all a little older and wiser."

8

The walks across the park were not rituals of anticipation. The road bent west and he walked past the tennis courts without thinking much about the room where she'd be waiting or the bedroom down the hall. They took erotic pleasure from each other but this is not what sent him back there. It was what they knew together, in the timeless drift of the long spiral down, and he went back again even if these meetings contradicted what he'd lately taken to be the truth of his life, that it was meant to be lived seriously and responsibly, not snatched in clumsy fistfuls.

Later she would say what someone always says.

"Do you have to leave?"

He would stand naked by the bed.

"I'll always have to leave."

"And I'll always have to make your leaving mean something else. Make it mean something romantic or sexy. But not empty, not lonely. Do I know how to do this?"

But she was not a contradiction, was she? She was not someone to be snatched at, not a denial of some truth he may have come upon in these long strange days and still nights, these after-days.

These are the days after. Everything now is measured by after.

She said, "Do I know how to make one thing out of another, without pretending? Can I stay who I am, or do I have to become all those other people who watch someone walk out the door? We're not other people, are we?"

But she would look at him in a way that made him feel he must be someone else, standing there by the bed, ready to say what someone always says.

They sat in a corner booth glaring at each other. Carol Shoup wore a striped silk overblouse, purple and white, that looked Moorish or Persian.

She said, "Under the circumstances, what do you expect?"

"I expect you to call and ask."

"But under the circumstances, how could I even bring up the subject?"

"But you did bring it up," Lianne said.

"Only after the fact. I couldn't ask you to edit such a book. After what happened to Keith, everything, all of it. I don't see how you'd want to get involved. A book that's so enormously immersed, going back on it, leading up to it. And a book that's so demanding, so incredibly tedious."

"A book you're publishing."

"We have to."

"After it's been making the rounds for how many years?"

"We have to. Four or five years," Carol said. "Because it seems to predict what happened."

"Seems to predict."

"Statistical tables, corporate reports, architectural blueprints, terrorist flow charts. What else?"

"A book you're publishing."

"It's badly written, badly organized and I would say deeply and enormously boring. Collected many rejections. Became a legend among agents and editors."

"A book you're publishing."

"Line-editing this beast."

"Who's the author?"

"A retired aeronautical engineer. We call him the Unaflyer. He doesn't live in a remote cabin with his bomb-making chemicals and his college yearbooks but he's been working obsessively for fifteen or sixteen years."

There was serious money to be made, by freelance standards, if a book was a major project. In this case it was also a rushed project, timely, newsworthy, even visionary, at least in the publisher's planned catalog copy—a book detailing a series of interlocking global forces that appeared to converge at an explosive point in time and space that might be said to represent the locus of Boston, New York and Washington on a late-summer morning early in the twenty-first century.

"Line-editing this beast could put you in traction for years to come. It's all data. It's all facts, maps and schedules."

"But it seems to predict."

The book needed a freelance editor, someone able to work long hours outside the scheduled frenzy of phone calls, e-mails, lunch dates and meetings that an in-house editor encountered—the frenzy that constitutes the job.

"It contains a long sort of treatise on plane hijacking. It contains many documents concerning the vulnerability of certain airports. It names Dulles and Logan. It names many things that actually happened or are happening now. Wall Street, Afghanistan, this thing, that thing. Afghanistan is happening."

Lianne didn't care how dense, raveled and intimidating the

material might be or how finally unprophetic. This is what she wanted. She didn't know she wanted this until Carol mentioned the book, derisively, in passing. She thought she'd been invited to lunch to discuss an assignment. It turned out that the meeting was strictly personal. Carol wanted to talk about Keith. The only book Carol mentioned was precisely the one not intended for Lianne and precisely the one that Lianne needed to edit.

"Do you want dessert?"

"No."

Stand apart. See things clinically, unemotionally. This is what Martin had told her. Measure the elements. Work the elements together. Learn something from the event. Make yourself equal to it.

Carol wanted to talk about Keith, hear about Keith. She wanted the man's story, their story, back together, moment by moment. The blouse she was wearing belonged to another body type, another skin color, a knockoff of a Persian or Moroccan robe. Lianne noticed this. She had nothing interesting to tell this woman about Keith because nothing interesting had happened that was not too intimate for telling.

"Do you want coffee?"

"I hit a woman in the face the other day."

"What for?"

"What do you hit people for?"

"Wait. You hit a woman?"

"They make you mad. That's what for."

Carol was looking at her.

"Do you want coffee?"

"No."

"You have your husband back. Your son has a father full-time."

"You don't know anything."

"Show some happiness, some relief, something. Show something."

"It's only beginning. Don't you know that?"

"You have him back."

"You don't know anything," she said.

The waiter stood nearby, waiting for someone to ask for the check.

"All right, look. If something happens," Carol said. "Like the editor can't deal with the material. The editor can't work fast enough. She feels this book is destroying the life she has carefully built over the last twenty-seven years. I'll call you."

"Call me," Lianne said. "Otherwise don't call me."

After that day, when she could not remember where she lived, Rosellen S. did not come back to the group.

The members wanted to write about her and Lianne watched them at work, folded over their legal pads. Now and then a head would lift, someone staring into a memory or a word. All the words for what is inevitable seemed to crowd the room and she found herself thinking of the old passport photos on the wall of her mother's apartment, from Martin's collection, faces looking out of a sepia distance, lost in time.

The agent's circular stamp at the corner of a photo.

The bearer's status and port of embarkation.

Royaume de Bulgarie.

Embassy of the Hashemite Kingdom.

Türkiye Cumhuriyeti.

She'd begun to see the people before her, Omar, Carmen and the others, in the same isolated setting, with the signature of the bearer sometimes written across the photo itself, a woman in a cloche, a younger woman who looked Jewish, *Staatsange-*

hörigkeit, her face and eyes showing deeper meaning than an ocean crossing alone might account for, and the woman's face that's almost lost in shadow, the printed word *Napoli* curled around the border of a circular stamp.

Pictures snapped anonymously, images rendered by machine. There was something in the premeditation of these photographs, the bureaucratic intent, the straightforward poses that brought her paradoxically into the lives of the subjects. Maybe what she saw was human ordeal set against the rigor of the state. She saw people fleeing, there to here, with darkest hardship pressing the edges of the frame. Thumbprints, emblems with tilted crosses, man with handlebar mustache, girl in braids. She thought she was probably inventing a context. She didn't know anything about the people in the photographs. She only knew the photographs. This is where she found innocence and vulnerability, in the nature of old passports, in the deep texture of the past itself, people on long journeys, people now dead. Such beauty in faded lives, she thought, in images, words, languages, signatures, stamped advisories.

Cyrillic, Greek, Chinese.

Dati e connotati del Titolare.

Les Pays Etrangers.

She watches the members write about Rosellen S. A head lifts, then drops, and they sit and write. She knows they are not looking out of a tinted mist, as the passport bearers are, but receding into one. Another head comes up and then another and she tries not to catch the eye of either individual. Soon they would all look up. For the first time since the sessions began, she is afraid to hear what they will say when they read from the ruled sheets.

―――――

He stood near the front of the large room watching them work out. They were in their twenties and thirties, arrayed in ranks on the stair climbers and elliptical trainers. He walked along the near aisle, feeling a bond with these men and women, not sure quite why. They strained against weighted metal sleds and rode stationary bikes. There were rowing machines and spidery isotonic devices. He paused at the entrance to the weight room and saw powerlifters fixed between safety bars, grunting up out of their squats. He saw women at the speed bags nearby, throwing hooks and jabs, and others doing footwork drills, skipping rope, one leg tucked up, arms crossed.

An escort was with him, young man in white, on the staff of the fitness center. Keith stood at the rear of the great open space, people everywhere in motion, blood pumping. They quick-walked on the treadmills or ran in place, never seeming regimented, never rigidly linked. It was a scene charged with purpose and a kind of elemental sex, rooted sex, women arched and bent, all elbows and knees, neck veins jutting. But there was something else as well. These were the people he knew, if he knew anyone. Here, together, these were the ones he could stand with in the days after. Maybe that's what he was feeling, a spirit, a kinship of trust.

He walked down the far aisle, escort trailing, waiting for Keith to ask a question. He was looking the place over. He would need to do serious gymwork once he started his job, days away now. It was no good spending eight hours at the office, ten hours, then going straight home. He would need to burn things off, test his body, direct himself inward, working on his strength, stamina, agility, sanity. He would need an offsetting discipline, a form of controlled behavior, voluntary, that kept him from shambling into the house hating everybody.

Her mother was asleep again. Lianne wanted to go home but knew she couldn't. It was only five minutes ago that Martin had walked out the door, abruptly, and she didn't want Nina to wake up alone. She went to the kitchen and found some fruit and cheese. She stood at the sink washing a pear and heard something in the living room. She turned off the faucet and listened and then went into the room. Her mother was talking to her.

"I have dreams when I'm not quite asleep, not all the way down, and I'm dreaming."

"We need to have some lunch, both of us."

"I almost feel I can open my eyes and see what I'm dreaming. Makes no sense, does it? The dream is not so much in my mind as all around me."

"It's the pain medication. You're taking too much, for no reason."

"The physical therapy causes pain."

"You're not doing the physical therapy."

"This must mean I'm not taking the medication."

"That's not funny. One of those drugs you take is habit-forming. At least one."

"Where's my grandson?"

"Exactly where he was last time you asked. But that's not the question. The question is Martin."

"It's hard to imagine that a day will come anytime soon when we stop arguing about this."

"He was very intense."

"You haven't seen him when he's intense. It's a lingering thing, goes back years, well before we knew each other."

"Which is twenty years, yes."

"Yes."

"But before that, what?"

"He was involved in the times. All that turmoil. He was active."

"Bare walls. The art investor with bare walls."

"Nearly bare. Yes, that's Martin."

"Martin Ridnour."

"Yes."

"Did you tell me once that's not his real name?"

"I'm not sure. Maybe," Nina said.

"If I heard it, then it came from you. Is that his real name?"

"No."

"I don't think you told me his real name."

"Maybe I don't know his real name."

"Twenty years."

"Not continuously. Not even for prolonged periods. He's somewhere, I'm somewhere else."

"He has a wife."

"She's somewhere else too."

"Twenty years. Traveling with him. Sleeping with him."

"Why do I have to know his name? He's Martin. What will I know about him if I know his name that I don't know now?"

"You'll know his name."

"He's Martin."

"You'll know his name. This is nice to know."

Her mother nodded toward the two paintings on the north wall.

"When we first knew each other I talked to him about Giorgio Morandi. Showed him a book. Beautiful still lifes. Form, color, depth. He was just getting started in the business and barely knew Morandi's name. Went to Bologna to see the work firsthand. Came back saying no, no, no, no. Minor artist. Empty, self-involved, bourgeois. Basically a Marxist critique, this is what Martin delivered."

"Twenty years later."

"He sees form, color, depth, beauty."

"Is this an advance in aesthetics?"

"He sees the light."

"Or a sellout, a self-deception. Remarks of a property owner."

"He sees the light," Nina said.

"He also sees the money. These are very pricey objects."

"Yes, they are. And at first, quite seriously, I wondered how he'd acquired them. I suspect in those early years he sometimes dealt in stolen art."

"Interesting fellow."

"He said to me once, I've done some things. He said, This doesn't make my life more interesting than yours. It can be made to sound more interesting. But in memory, in those depths, he said, there is not much vivid color or wild excitement. It is all gray and waiting. Sitting, waiting. He said, It is all sort of neutral, you know."

She did the accent with a deft edge, maybe a little nasty.

"What was he waiting for?"

"History, I think. The call to action. The visit from the police."

"Which branch of the police?"

"Not the art-theft squad. I know one thing. He was a member of a collective in the late nineteen sixties. Kommune One. Demonstrating against the German state, the fascist state. That's how they saw it. First they threw eggs. Then they set off bombs. After that I'm not sure what he did. I think he was in Italy for a while, in the turmoil, when the Red Brigades were active. But I don't know."

"You don't know."

"No."

"Twenty years. Eating and sleeping together. You don't know. Did you ask him? Did you press him?"

"He showed me a poster once, a few years ago, when I saw

him in Berlin. He keeps an apartment there. A wanted poster. German terrorists of the early seventies. Nineteen names and faces."

"Nineteen."

"Wanted for murder, bombings, bank robberies. He keeps it—I don't know why he keeps it. But I know why he showed it to me. He's not one of the faces on the poster."

"Nineteen."

"Men and women. I counted. He may have been part of a support group or a sleeper cell. I don't know."

"You don't know."

"He thinks these people, these jihadists, he thinks they have something in common with the radicals of the sixties and seventies. He thinks they're all part of the same classical pattern. They have their theorists. They have their visions of world brotherhood."

"Do they make him nostalgic?"

"Don't think I won't bring this up."

"Bare walls. Nearly bare, you said. Is this part of the old longing? Days and nights in seclusion, hiding out somewhere, renouncing every trace of material comfort. Maybe he killed someone. Did you ask him? Did you press him on this?"

"Look, if he'd done something serious, causing death or injury, do you think he'd be walking around today? He's not in hiding anymore, if he ever was. He's here, there and everywhere."

"Operating under a false name," Lianne said.

She was on the sofa, facing her mother, watching her. She'd never detected a weakness in Nina, none that she could recall, some frailty of character or compromise of hard clear judgment. She found herself prepared to take advantage and this surprised her. She was ready to bleed the moment, bearing in, ripping in.

"All these years. Never forcing the issue. Look at the man

147

he's become, the man we know. Isn't this the kind of man they would have seen as the enemy? Those men and women on the wanted poster. Kidnap the bastard. Burn his paintings."

"Oh I think he knows this. Don't you think he knows this?"

"But what do you know? Don't you pay a price for not knowing?"

"It's my price. Shut up," her mother said.

She drew a cigarette from the pack and held it. She seemed to be thinking into some distant matter, not remembering so much as measuring, marking the reach or degree of something, the meaning of something.

"The one wall that holds an object is in Berlin."

"The wanted poster."

"The poster does not hang. He keeps the poster in a closet, in a mailing tube. No, it's a small photograph in a plain frame, hanging over his bed. He and I, a snapshot. We're standing before a church in one of the hill towns in Umbria. We'd met only a day earlier. He asked a woman walking by to take our picture."

"Why do I hate this story?"

"His name is Ernst Hechinger. You hate this story because you think it shames me. Makes me complicit in a maudlin gesture, a pathetic gesture. Foolish little snapshot. The one object he displays."

"Have you tried to determine whether this man Ernst Hechinger is wanted by the police somewhere in Europe? Just to know. To stop saying I don't know."

She wanted to punish her mother but not for Martin or not just for that. It was nearer and deeper and finally about one thing only. This is what everything was about, who they were, the fierce clasp, like hands bound in prayer, now and evermore.

Nina lit the cigarette and exhaled. She made it seem an effort to do this, breathe out smoke. She was drowsy again. One of her medications contained codeine phosphate and she was careful when taking it until recently. It was only days in fact, a week or so, since she'd stopped following the exercise regimen without altering her intake of painkillers. Lianne believed that this slackness of will was a defeat that had Martin in the middle of it. These were his nineteen, these hijackers, these jihadists, even if only in her mother's mind.

"What are you working on?"

"Book on ancient alphabets. All the forms writing took, all the materials they used."

"Sounds interesting."

"You ought to read this book."

"Sounds interesting."

"Interesting, demanding, deeply enjoyable at times. Drawing as well. Pictorial writing. I'll get you a copy when it's published."

"Pictograms, hieroglyphics, cuneiform," her mother said.

She appeared to be dreaming aloud.

She said, "Sumerians, Assyrians, so on."

"I'll get you a copy, definitely."

"Thank you."

"You're welcome," Lianne said.

The cheese and fruit were on a platter in the kitchen. She sat with her mother a moment longer and then went in to get the food.

Three of the cardplayers were called by last name only, Dockery, Rumsey, Hovanis, and two by first name, Demetrius and Keith. Terry Cheng was Terry Cheng.

Someone told Rumsey one night, it was Dockery the waggish adman, that everything in his life would be different, Rumsey's, if one letter in his name was different. An *a* for the *u*.

Making him, effectively, Ramsey. It was the *u*, the *rum*, that had shaped his life and mind. The way he walks and talks, his slouchings, his very size and shape, the slowness and thickness that pour off him, the way he puts his hand down his shirt to scratch an itch. This would all be different if he'd been born a Ramsey.

They sat waiting for R's reply, watching him linger in the aura of his defined state.

She went down to the basement with a basket full of laundry. There was a small gray room, damp and stale, with a washer and dryer and a metallic chill that she felt in her teeth.

She heard the dryer in operation and walked in to see Elena leaning on the wall with her arms folded and a cigarette in her hand. Elena did not look up.

For a moment they listened to the load bounce around the drum. Then Lianne put her basket down and raised the lid of the washer. The filter pan held the lint rubble of the other woman's wash.

She looked at it briefly, then took the pan out of the washer and extended it to Elena. The woman paused, then took it and looked. Without changing position she used a backhand motion to bang the pan twice against the lower part of the wall she was leaning on. She looked at it again, took a drag on her cigarette and handed the pan across to Lianne, who took it and looked and then placed it on top of the dryer. She threw her things in the washer, fistfuls of darks, and put the filter pan back on the agitator or activator or whatever it was called. She poured in detergent, made selections on the control panel, set the dial on the other side of the panel and closed the lid. Then she pulled the control knob to start the wash.

But she didn't leave the room. She assumed the load in the

dryer was nearly done or why would the woman be standing here waiting. She assumed the woman had come down only minutes ago, saw the load was not yet done and decided to wait rather than go up and down and up again. She couldn't see the time dial clearly from this position and preferred not to make a show of looking. But she had no intention of leaving the room. She stood against the wall adjacent to the wall the woman was leaning on, half slouched. Their straitened lanes of vision possibly crossed somewhere near the middle of the room. She kept her back erect, feeling the impress of the old pocked wall against her shoulder blades.

The washer began to rumble, the dryer tossed and clicked, shirt buttons hitting the drum. There was no question that she would outwait the other woman. The question was what the woman would do with the cigarette if she finished smoking it before the load was done. The question was whether they'd look at each other before the woman left the room. The room was like a monk's cell with a pair of giant prayer wheels beating out a litany. The question was whether a look would lead to words and then what.

It was a rainy Monday in the world and she walked over to Godzilla Apartments, where the kid was spending an after-school hour with the Siblings, playing video games.

She used to write poetry on days like this when she was in school. There was something about rain and poetry. Later there would be something about rain and sex. The poems were usually about the rain, how it felt to be indoors watching the lonely drops slide down the windowpane.

Her umbrella was useless in the wind. It was the kind of wind-whipped rain that empties the streets of people and makes

day and place feel anonymous. This was the weather everywhere, the state of mind, generic Monday, and she walked very
close to buildings and ran across streets and felt the wind hit
straight down when she reached the redbrick heights of Godzilla.

She had a quick cup of coffee with the mother, Isabel, and
then peeled her son off the computer screen and muscled him
into his jacket. He wanted to stay, they wanted him to stay. She
told them she was a villain too real for video games.

Katie followed them to the door. She wore red jeans rolled
up and a pair of suede ankle boots that glowed neon along the
welt when she walked. Her brother Robert hung back, a dark-
eyed boy who looked too shy to speak, eat, walk a dog.

The telephone rang.

Lianne said to the girl, "You're not still sky-watching, are
you? Searching the skies day and night? No. Or are you?"

The girl looked at Justin and smiled in sly connivance, saying
nothing.

"He won't tell me," Lianne said. "I ask and ask."

He said, "No, you don't."

"But if I did, you wouldn't tell me."

Katie's eyes went brighter. She was enjoying this, alert to the
prospect of a crafty reply. Her mother was talking on the wall-
mounted phone in the kitchen.

Lianne said to the girl, "Still waiting for word? Still watching
for planes? Day and night at the window? No. I don't believe it."

She leaned toward the girl, speaking in a stage whisper.

"Still talking to that person? The man whose name some of
us are not supposed to know."

The brother looked stricken. He stood fifteen feet behind
Katie, dead still, looking at the parquet floor between his sister's
boots.

"Is he still out there, somewhere, making you search the

skies? The man whose name maybe we all know even if some of us are not supposed to know."

Justin plucked her jacket away from her elbow, which meant let's go home now.

"Maybe just maybe. This is what I think. Maybe it's time for him to disappear. The man whose name we all know."

She had her hands on Katie's face, cradling it, caging it, ear to ear. In the kitchen the mother was raising her voice, talking about a credit-card problem.

"Maybe it's time. Do you think that's possible? Maybe you're just not interested anymore. Yes or no? Maybe just maybe it's time to stop searching the skies, time to stop talking about the man I'm talking about. What do you think? Yes or no?"

The girl looked less happy now. She tried to dart a look left to Justin, like what's going on here, but Lianne pressed a little tighter and used her right hand to block the view, smiling at the girl mock-playfully.

The brother was trying to will his invisibility. They were confused and a little scared but that's not why she took her hands from Katie's face. She was ready to leave, that's why, and all the way down on the elevator, twenty-seventh floor to lobby, she thought of the mythical figure who'd said the planes were coming back, the man whose name they all knew. But she'd forgotten it.

Rain was lighter now, wind diminished. They walked without a word. She tried to remember the name but could not do it. The kid would not walk beneath the spread umbrella, staying four paces back. It was an easy name, this much she knew, but the easy names were the ones that killed her.

9

This day, beyond others, she found it hard to leave. She came out of the community center and walked west, thinking about another day, not long in coming, when the storyline sessions would have to end. The group was reaching that time and she didn't think she could do it again, start over, six or seven people, the ballpoint pens and writing pads, the beauty of it, yes, the way they sing their lives, but also the unwariness they bring to what they know, the strange brave innocence of it, and her own grasping after her father.

She wanted to walk home and when she got there she wanted to find a phone message from Carol Shoup. Call me soonest please. It was only a feeling but she trusted it and knew what the message would mean, that the editor had quit the assignment. She would walk in the door, listen to the four-word message and know that the editor could not handle the book, a text so webbed in obsessive detail that it was impossible to proceed further. She wanted to walk in the door and see the lighted number on the telephone. This is Carol, call me soonest. A six-word message that implied a great deal more. This is what Carol liked to say in her phone messages. Call me soonest. It was something promised, that last urgent word, an indication of auspicious circumstance.

She walked without plan, west on 116th Street past the barbershop and record shop, the fruit markets and bakery. She turned south for five blocks and then glanced to her right and saw the high wall of weathered granite that supported the elevated tracks, where trains carry commuters to and from the city. She thought at once of Rosellen S. but didn't know why. She walked in that direction and came to a building marked Greater Highway Deliverance Temple. She paused a moment, absorbing the name and noticing the ornate pilasters above the entrance and the stone cross at roof's edge. There was a sign out front listing the temple's activities. Sunday school, Sunday morning glory, Friday deliverance service and Bible study. She stood and thought. She thought of the conversation with Dr. Apter concerning the day when Rosellen could not remember where she lived. This was an occasion that haunted Lianne, the breathless moment when things fall away, streets, names, all sense of direction and location, every fixed grid of memory. Now she understood why Rosellen seemed to be a presence in this street. Here was the place, this temple whose name was a hallelujah shout, where she'd found refuge and assistance.

Again she stood and thought. She thought of the language that Rosellen had been using at the last sessions she'd been able to attend, how she developed extended versions of a single word, all the inflections and connectives, a kind of protection perhaps, a gathering against the last bare state, where even the deepest moan may not be grief but only moan.

Do we say goodbye, yes, going, am going, will be going, the last time go, will go.

This is what she was able to recall from the limp script of Rosellen's last pages.

156

He walked back through the park. The runners seemed eternal, circling the reservoir, and he tried not to think of the last half hour, with Florence, talking into her silence. This was another kind of eternity, the stillness in her face and body, outside time.

He picked up the kid at school and then walked north into a breeze that carried a faint stir of rain. He was relieved to have something to talk about, Justin's schoolwork, his friends and teachers.

"Where do we go?"

"Your mother said she'd be walking home from the meeting uptown. We want to intercept her."

"Why?"

"To surprise her. Sneak up on her. Lift her spirits."

"How do we know which way she will come?"

"That's the challenge. A direct route, an indirect route, she's walking fast, she's walking slow."

He was speaking into the breeze, not quite to Justin. He was still back there, with Florence, double in himself, coming and going, the walks across the park and back, the deep shared self, down through the smoke, and then here again to safety and family, to the implications of one's conduct.

In one hundred days or so, he would be forty years old. This was his father's age. His father was forty, his uncles. They would always be forty, looking aslant at him. How is it possible that he was about to become someone of clear and distinct definition, husband and father, finally, occupying a room in three dimensions in the manner of his parents?

He'd stood by the window in those last minutes looking at the opposite wall, where a photograph hung, Florence as a girl, in a white dress, with her mother and father.

The kid said, "We go which way? This street or that street?"

It was a picture he'd barely noticed before and the sight of her in that setting, untouched by the consequences of what he'd come to say, caused a tightness in his chest. What she needed in him was his seeming calm, even if she didn't understand it. He knew she was grateful for this, the fact that he was able to read the levels of her distress. He was the still figure, watching, ever attentive, saying little. This is what she wanted to cling to. But now she was the one who would not speak, watching him by the window, hearing the soft voice that tells her it is ended now.

Understand, he said.

Because what else finally was there to say? He watched the light fall from her face. This was the old undoing that was always near, now come inevitably into her life again, an injury no less painful for being fated.

She stood a moment longer outside the temple. There were voices in the schoolyard up ahead, across the street from the ele-vated tracks. A crossing guard stood at the corner, arms folded, with sparse traffic along the narrow one-way stretch between the sidewalk and the rampart of scarred stone blocks.

A train flew by.

She walked toward the corner, knowing there would be no message waiting when she got home. It was gone now, the sense that a message would be waiting. Three words. Call me soonest. She'd told Carol not to call unless she could deliver the book in question. There was no book, not for her.

A train went by, southbound this time, and she heard some-one call in Spanish.

There was a row of apartment buildings, the projects, situated on this side of the tracks, and when she reached the corner she looked to her right, past the schoolyard, and saw the jutting facade of one wing of a building, heads in windows, half a dozen maybe, up around the ninth, tenth, eleventh floors, and she heard the voice again, someone calling out, a woman, and saw the schoolkids, some of them, pausing in their games, looking up and around.

A teacher walked slowly toward the fence, tall man, swinging a whistle on a string.

She waited at the corner. There were more voices now from the projects and she looked that way again, noting their line of sight. They were looking down at the tracks, northbound side, to a point almost directly above her. Then she saw the students, some of them backing across the yard toward the wall of the school building, and she understood they were trying to get a better view of this side of the tracks.

A car went by, radio blasting.

It took a moment for him to come into view, upper body only, a man on the other side of the protective fence that bordered the tracks. He wasn't a track worker in a blaze orange vest. She saw that much. She saw him from the chest up and heard the schoolkids now, calling to each other, all the games in suspension.

He seemed to be coming out of nowhere. There was no station stop here, no ticket office or platform for passengers, and she had no idea how he'd managed to gain access to the track area. White male, she thought. White shirt, dark jacket.

The immediate street was quiet. People passing looked and walked and a few stopped, briefly, and others, younger, lingered. It was the kids in the schoolyard who were interested and the faces high to her right, more of them now, floating in the windows of the projects.

White male in suit and tie, it now appeared, as he made his way down the short ladder through an opening in the fence.

This is when she knew, of course. She watched him lower himself to the maintenance platform that jutted over the street, just south of the intersection. This is when she understood, although she'd felt something even before her first glimpse of the figure. There were the faces in the high windows, something about the faces, a forewarning, the way you know something before you perceive it directly. This is who he had to be.

He stood on the platform, about three stories above her. Everything was painted brownish rust, the upper tiers of coarse granite, the barrier he'd just passed through and the platform itself, a slatted metal structure resembling a large fire escape, twelve feet long and six wide, accessible normally to workers on the tracks or those at street level arriving in a maintenance truck equipped with vertical boom and open bucket.

A train went by, southbound again. Why is he doing this, she thought.

He was thinking, not listening. He began to listen as they made their way uptown, talking in brief sprints, and he realized that the kid was using monosyllables again.

He told him, "Cut the crap."

"What?"

"How's that for monosyllables?"

"What?"

"Cut the crap," he said.

"What for? You tell me I don't talk."

"That's your mother, not me."

"Now I talk, you tell me not to talk."

He was getting better at this, Justin was, barely pausing between words. At first it was an instructive form of play but the practice carried something else now, a solemn obstinacy, nearly ritualistic.

"Look, I don't care. You can talk in the Inuit language if you

like. Learn Inuit. They have an alphabet of syllables instead of letters. You can speak one syllable at a time. It'll take you a minute
and a half to say one long word. I'm in no hurry. Take all the time
you want. Long pauses between the syllables. We'll eat whale
blubber and you can speak Inuit."

"I do not think I would like to eat whale meat."

"It's not meat, it's blubber."

"This is the same as fat."

"Say blubber."

"This is the same as fat. It is fat. Whale fat."

Wise-ass little kid.

"The point is that your mother doesn't like you talking this
way. It upsets her. We want to give her a break. You can understand this. And even if you can't understand it, don't do it."

The mixed skies were darker now. He began to think this was
a bad idea, trying to meet her coming home. They went east a
block, then north again.

There was something else he thought concerning Lianne. He
thought he would tell her about Florence. It was the right thing
to do. It was the kind of perilous truth that would lead to an
understanding of clean and even proportions, long-lasting, with
a feeling of reciprocal love and trust. He believed this. It was a
way to stop being double in himself, trailing the taut shadow of
what is unsaid.

He would tell her about Florence. She would say she knew
something was going on but in view of the completely uncommon nature of the involvement, with its point of origin in smoke
and fire, this is not an unforgivable offense.

He would tell her about Florence. She would say she could
understand the intensity of the involvement, in view of the
completely uncommon nature of its origin, in smoke and fire,
and this would cause her to suffer enormously.

He would tell her about Florence. She would get a steak knife and kill him.

He would tell her about Florence. She would enter a period of long and tortured withdrawal.

He would tell her about Florence. She would say, After we've just renewed our marriage. She would say, After the terrifying day of the planes has brought us together again. How could the same terror? She would say, How could the same terror threaten everything we've felt for each other, everything I've felt these past weeks?

He would tell her about Florence. She would say, I want to meet her.

He would tell her about Florence. Her periodic insomnia would become total, requiring a course of treatment that includes diet, medication and psychiatric counseling.

He would tell her about Florence. She would spend more time at her mother's apartment, accompanied by the kid, remaining there well into evening and leaving Keith to wander empty rooms on his return from the office, as in the meager seasons of his exile.

He would tell her about Florence. She would want to be convinced that it was over and he would convince her because it was true, simply and forever.

He would tell her about Florence. She would send him to hell with a look and then call a lawyer.

She heard the sound and looked to her right. A boy in the schoolyard was dribbling a basketball. The sound did not belong to the moment but he wasn't playing, only walking, taking the basketball with him, absently bouncing it as he walked toward the fence, head up, eyes on the figure above.

Others followed. With the man in full view now, students advanced from the far end of the yard toward the fence. The man had affixed the safety harness to the rail of the platform. The students advanced from every point of the schoolyard to get a closer look at what was happening.

She moved back. She moved the other way, backing into the building that stood on the corner. Then she looked around for someone, just to exchange a glance. She looked for the crossing guard, who was nowhere in sight. She wished she could believe this was some kind of antic street theater, an absurdist drama that provokes onlookers to share a comic understanding of what is irrational in the great schemes of being or in the next small footstep.

This was too near and deep, too personal. All she wanted to share was a look, catch someone's eye, see what she herself was feeling. She did not think of walking away. He was right above her but she wasn't watching and wasn't walking away. She looked at the teacher across the street, whistle pressed in one fist, string dangling, his other hand gripping the strands of the chain-link fence. She heard someone above her, in the apartment building that occupied the corner, a woman at the window.

She said, "What you doing?"

Her voice came from a point somewhere above the level of the maintenance platform. Lianne didn't look. The street to her left was empty except for a ragged man coming out of the archway beneath the tracks, carrying a bicycle wheel in his hand. This is where she looked. Then, again, the woman's voice.

She said, "I call nine one one."

Lianne tried to understand why he was here and not somewhere else. These were strictly local circumstances, people in windows, some kids in a schoolyard. Falling Man was known to appear among crowds or at sites where crowds might quickly form. Here was an old derelict rolling a wheel down the street. Here was a woman in a window, having to ask who he was.

Other voices now, from the projects and the schoolyard, and she looked up again. He stood balanced on the rail of the platform. The rail had a broad flat top and he stood there, blue suit, white shirt, blue tie, black shoes. He loomed over the sidewalk, legs spread slightly, arms out from his body and bent at the elbows, asymmetrically, man in fear, looking out of some deep pool of concentration into lost space, dead space.

She slipped around the corner of the building. It was a senseless gesture of flight, adding only a couple of yards to the distance between them, but then it wasn't so odd, not if he truly fell, if the harness did not hold. She watched him, her shoulder jammed to the brick wall of the building. She did not think of turning and leaving.

They all waited. But he did not fall. He stood poised on the rail for a full minute, then another. The woman's voice was louder now.

She said, "You don't be here."

Kids called out, they shouted inevitably, "*Jump*," but only two or three and then it stopped and there were voices from the projects, mournful calls in the damp air.

Then she began to understand. Performance art, yes, but he wasn't here to perform for those at street level or in the high windows. He was situated where he was, remote from station personnel and railroad police, waiting for a train to come, northbound, this is what he wanted, an audience in motion, passing scant yards from his standing figure.

She thought of the passengers. The train would bust out of the tunnel south of here and then begin to slow down, approaching the station at 125th Street, three-quarters of a mile ahead. It would pass and he would jump. There would be those aboard who see him standing and those who see him jump, all jarred out of their reveries or their newspapers or muttering stunned into their cell phones. These people had not seen him attach the safety harness. They would only see him fall out of sight. Then, she thought, the ones already speaking into phones, the others groping for phones, all would try to describe what they've seen or what others nearby have seen and are now trying to describe to them.

There was one thing for them to say, essentially. Someone falling. Falling man. She wondered if this was his intention, to spread the word this way, by cell phone, intimately, as in the towers and in the hijacked planes.

Or she was dreaming his intentions. She was making it up, stretched so tight across the moment that she could not think her own thoughts.

"I'll tell you what I'm trying to do," he said.

They passed a supermarket window splashed with broadsheets. The kid had his hands hidden in his sleeves.

"I'm trying to read her mind. Will she walk down one of the avenues, First, Second, Third, or wander a little, here and there?"

"You said this already."

It was something he'd been doing lately, extending the sleeves of his sweater to cover his hands. Each hand was closed into a fist and this allowed him to use his fingertips to secure the sleeve to the hand. Sometimes a thumb tip protruded and a trace of knuckles.

"I said this. All right. But I didn't say I was going to read her mind. Read her mind," he said, "and tell me what you think."

"Maybe she changed her mind. She's in a taxi."

He wore a backpack to carry his books and school supplies,

which left his hands free to be concealed. It was a mannerism that Keith associated with older boys who try to be noticeably peculiar.

"She said she'd walk."

"Maybe she took the subway."

"She doesn't take the subway anymore. She said she'd walk."

"What's wrong with the subway?"

He noted the mood of somber opposition, the drag in the kid's gait. They walked west now, somewhere below 100th Street, stopping at each intersection to peer uptown, trying to spot her among the faces and shapes. Justin pretended to lose interest, drifting toward the curb to study the dust and lesser debris. He didn't like being deprived of his monosyllabic powers.

"There's nothing wrong with the subway," Keith said. "Maybe you're right. Maybe she took the subway."

He would tell her about Florence. She would look at him and wait. He would tell her it was not, in truth, the kind of relationship that people refer to when they use the word *affair*. It was not an affair. There was sex, yes, but not romance. There was emotion, yes, but generated by external conditions he could not control. She would say nothing and wait. He would say that the time he'd spent with Florence was already beginning to seem an aberration—that was the word. It was the kind of thing, he'd say, that a person looks back on with a sense of having entered something that was, in truth, unreal, and he was already feeling this and knowing this. She would sit and look at him. He would mention the brevity of the thing, the easily countable occasions. He was not a trial lawyer but still, technically, a lawyer, even if he barely believed it himself, and he would assess his guilt openly and present the facts attending the brief relationship and include those crucial circumstances so often and aptly described as extenuating. She would sit in the chair no one ever sat in, the mahogany side chair set against the wall between the desk and the bookshelves, and he would look at her and wait.

"She's probably already home," the kid said, walking with one foot in the gutter and one up on the curb.

They went past a pharmacy and a travel agency. Keith saw something up ahead. He marked the stride of a woman crossing the street, uncertainly, near the intersection. She seemed to stop in midcrossing. A taxi obscured his view for a moment but he knew that something was wrong. He leaned over and gave the kid a backhand tap on the upper arm, keeping his eyes on the figure ahead. By the time she reached the corner on this side of the street, they were both running toward her.

She heard the train coming along the northbound track and watched him tense his body in preparation. The sound was a deep bass roll with an in-and-out recurrence, discrete not continuous, like pulsing numbers, and she could almost count the tenths of seconds as it grew louder.

The man stared into the brickwork of the corner building but did not see it. There was a blankness in his face, but deep, a kind of lost gaze. Because what was he doing finally? Because did he finally know? She thought the bare space he stared into must be his own, not some grim vision of others falling. But why was she standing here watching? Because she saw her husband somewhere near. She saw his friend, the one she'd met, or the other, maybe, or made him up and saw him, in a high window with smoke flowing out. Because she felt compelled, or only helpless, gripping the strap of her shoulder bag.

The train comes slamming through and he turns his head and looks into it (into his death by fire) and then brings his head back around and jumps.

Jumps or falls. He keels forward, body rigid, and falls full-length, headfirst, drawing a rustle of awe from the schoolyard with isolated cries of alarm that are only partly smothered by the passing roar of the train.

She felt her body go limp. But the fall was not the worst of it. The jolting end of the fall left him upside-down, secured to the harness, twenty feet above the pavement. The jolt, the sort of midair impact and bounce, the recoil, and now the stillness, arms at his sides, one leg bent at the knee. There was something awful about the stylized pose, body and limbs, his signature stroke. But the worst of it was the stillness itself and her nearness to the man, her position here, with no one closer to him than she was. She could have spoken to him but that was another plane of being, beyond reach. He remained motionless, with the train still running in a blur in her mind and the echoing deluge of sound falling about him, blood rushing to his head, away from hers.

She looked directly overhead and saw no sign of the woman in the window. She moved now, keeping to the side of the building, head down, feeling her way by hand along the rough surface of the masonry. His eyes were open but she guided herself by hand and then, once beyond the dangling figure, veered toward the middle of the sidewalk, moving quickly now.

Almost at once she came upon the derelict, the old thread-bare man, and he stood looking past her at the figure upended in midair. He seemed to be in a pose of his own, attached to this spot for half a lifetime, one papery hand clutching his bicycle wheel. His face showed an intense narrowing of thought and possibility. He was seeing something elaborately different from what he encountered step by step in the ordinary run of hours. He had to learn how to see it correctly, find a crack in the world where it might fit.

He didn't see her when she went by. She couldn't seem to

walk quickly enough, passing more projects or the same spreading development, one street and then another. She kept her head down, seeing things as fleeting shimmers, a coil of razor wire atop a low fence or a police cruiser going north, the way she'd come, a blue-white flare with faces. This made her think of him back there, suspended, body set in place, and she could not think beyond this.

She found she was running now, shoulder bag bouncing against her hip. She kept the things they wrote, the early-stage members, placing the pages in a binder in her shoulder bag to be hole-punched and fitted in the rings when she got home. The street was nearly empty, a warehouse to her left. She thought of the police cruiser coming to a stop directly under the fallen man. She ran at a fair clip, the pages in the binder and the names of the members skimming through her mind, first name and first letter of last name, this was how she knew them and saw them, and the shoulder bag keeping time, knocking against her hip, giving her a tempo, a rhythm to maintain. She was running level with the trains now and then above them, running uphill into a ribbed sky with taller bundled clouds bleeding down into the low array.

She thought, Died by his own hand.

She stopped running then and stood bent over, breathing heavily. She looked into the pavement. When she ran in the mornings she went long distances and never felt this drained and wasted. She was doubled over, like there were two of her, the one who'd done the running and the one who didn't know why. She waited for her breathing to ease and then stood upright. A couple of girls sat on a tenement stoop nearby, watching. She walked slowly to the top of the sloped street and then stopped again, remaining for some time with trains coming out of one hole and sinking into another, somewhere south of 100th Street.

She would take the pages home, the things they wrote, and place them with the earlier pages, hole-punched and fitted in the rings, numbering several hundred now. But first she would check the phone messages.

She crossed against the light and was standing on the crowded corner when she saw them coming toward her, running. They were bright and undisguised, moving past people wedged in routine anonymity. The sky seemed so near. They were bright with urgent life, that's why they were running, and she raised a hand so they might see her in the mass of faces, thirty-six days after the planes.

He had his Visa card, his frequent-flyer number. He had the use of the Mitsubishi. He'd lost twenty-two kilos and converted this to pounds, multiplying by 2.2046. The heat on the Gulf Coast was fierce at times and Hammad liked it. They rented a little stucco house on West Laurel Road and Amir turned down an offer of free cable TV. The house was pink. They sat around a table on day one and pledged to accept their duty, which was for each of them, in blood trust, to kill Americans.

Hammad pushed a cart through the supermarket. He was invisible to these people and they were becoming invisible to him. He looked at women sometimes, yes, the girl at the checkout named Meg or Peg. He knew things she could never in ten lifetimes begin to imagine. In the drenching light he saw a faint trace of fine soft silky down on her forearm and once he said something that made her smile.

His flight training was not going well. He sat rocking in the simulator and tried to match responses to conditions. The others, most of them, did better. There was always Amir of course. Amir flew small planes and logged extra hours in Boeing 767 simulators. He paid in cash at times, using money wired from Dubai. They thought the state would read their coded e-mails. The state would check out airline databases and all transactions involving certain sums of money. Amir did not concede this. He received certain sums of money wired to a Florida bank in his name, first and last, Mohamed Atta, because he was basically nobody from nowhere.

They were clean-shaven now. They wore T-shirts and cotton slacks. Hammad pushed his cart down the aisle to the checkout and when he said something she smiled but did not see him. The idea is to go unseen.

He knew his weight in pounds but did not announce it to the others or glorify it to himself. He converted meters to feet, multiplying by 3.28. There were two or three of them in the house and others came and went but not with the frequency or the burning spirit of the days on Marienstrasse. They were beyond that now, in full and determined preparation. Only Amir burned now. Amir was electric, dripping fire from the eyes.

The weight loss had come in Afghanistan, in a training camp, where Hammad had begun to understand that death is stronger than life. This is where the landscape consumed him, waterfalls frozen in space, a sky that never ended. It was all Islam, the rivers and streams. Pick up a stone and hold it in your fist, this is Islam. God's name on every tongue throughout the countryside. There was no feeling like this ever in his life. He wore a bomb vest and knew he was a man now, finally, ready to close the distance to God.

He drove the Mitsubishi down sleepy streets. One day, so strange, he saw a car with six or seven people crammed in, laughing and smoking, and they were young, maybe college kids, boys and girls. How easy would it be for him to walk out of his car and into theirs? Open the door with the car in motion and walk across the roadway to the other car, walk on air, and open the door of the other car and get in.

Amir switched from English to Arabic, quoting.

Never have We destroyed a nation whose term of life was not ordained beforehand.

This entire life, this world of lawns to water and hardware stacked on endless shelves, was total, forever, illusion. In the camp on the windy plain they were shaped into men. They fired weapons and set off explosives. They received instruction in the highest jihad, which is to make blood flow, their blood and that of others. People water lawns and eat fast food. Hammad ordered takeout at times, undeniably. Every day, five times, he prayed, sometimes less, sometimes not at all. He watched TV in a bar near the flight school and liked to imagine himself appearing on the screen, a videotaped figure walking through the gate-like detector on his way to the plane.

Not that they would ever get that far. The state had watch lists and undercover agents. The state knew how to read signals that flow out of your cell phone to microwave towers and orbiting satellites and into the cell phone of somebody in a car on a desert road in Yemen. Amir had stopped talking about Jews and Crusaders. It was all tactical now, plane schedules and fuel loads and getting men from one location to another, on time, in place.

These people jogging in the park, world domination. These old men who sit in beach chairs, veined white bodies and base-ball caps, they control our world. He wonders if they think of this, ever. He wonders if they see him standing here, clean-shaven, in tennis sneakers.

It was time to end all contact with his mother and father. He wrote them a letter and told them he would be traveling for a time. He worked for an engineering firm, he wrote, and would soon be promoted. He missed them, he wrote, and then tore up the letter and let the pieces drift away in a rip-tide of memories.

In the camp they gave him a long knife that had once belonged to a Saudi prince. An old man whipped the camel to its knees and then took the bridle and jerked the head skyward and Hammad slit the animal's throat. They made a noise when he did it, he and the camel both, braying, and he felt a deep warrior joy, standing back to watch the beast topple. He stood there, Hammad, arms spread wide, then kissed the bloody knife and raised it to the ones who were watching, the robed and turbaned men, showing his respect and gratitude.

One man on a visit did not know the name of the town they were in, outside another town called Venice. He'd forgotten the name or had never learned it. Hammad thought it didn't matter. Nokomis. What does it matter? Let these things fade into dust. Leave these things behind even as we sleep and eat here. All dust. Cars, houses, people. This is all a particle of dust in the fire and light of the days to come.

They passed through, one or two, now and then, and sometimes they told him about women they'd paid for sex, okay, but he didn't want to listen. He wanted to do this one thing right, of all the things he'd ever done. Here they were in the midst of unbelief, in the bloodstream of the *kufr*. They felt things together, he and his brothers. They felt the claim of danger and isolation. They felt the magnetic effect of plot. Plot drew them together more tightly than ever. Plot closed the world to the slenderest line of sight, where everything converges to a point. There was the claim of fate, that they were born to this. There was the claim of being chosen, out there, in the wind and sky of Islam. There was the statement that death made, the strongest claim of all, the highest jihad.

But does a man have to kill himself in order to accomplish something in the world?

They had simulator software. They played flight-simulator

games on their computer. The autopilot detects deviations from the route. The windshield is birdproof. He had a large cardboard illustration of the flight deck in a Boeing 767. He studied this in his room, memorizing the placement of levers and displays. The others called this poster his wife. He converted liters to gallons, grams to ounces. He sat in a barber chair and looked in the mirror. He was not here, it was not him.

He basically stopped changing his clothes. He wore the same shirt and trousers every day into the following week and underwear as well. He shaved but basically did not dress or undress, often sleeping in his clothes. The others made forceful comments. There was one time he took his clothes to the laundromat wearing someone else's clothes. He wore these clothes for a week and wanted the other man to wear his clothes now that they were clean, although clean or dirty didn't matter.

Wrong-eyed men and women laughing on TV, their military forces defiling the Land of the Two Holy Places.

Amir had made the pilgrimage to Mecca. He was a hajji, fulfilling the duty, saying the funeral prayer, *salat al-janaza*, claiming fellowship with those who'd died on the journey. Hammad did not feel deprived. They were soon to perform another kind of duty, unwritten, all of them, martyrs, together.

But does a man have to kill himself in order to count for something, be someone, find the way?

Hammad thought about this. He recalled what Amir had said. Amir thought clearly, in straight lines, direct and systematic.

Amir spoke in his face.

The end of our life is predetermined. We are carried toward that day from the minute we are born. There is no sacred law against what we are going to do. This is not suicide in any meaning or interpretation of the word. It is only something long written. We are finding the way already chosen for us.

You look at Amir and see a life too intense to last another minute, maybe because he never fucked a woman.

But what about this, Hammad thought. Never mind the man who takes his own life in this situation. What about the lives of the others he takes with him?

He was not eager to bring this up with Amir but did finally, the two of them alone in the house.

What about the others, those who will die?

Amir was impatient. He said they'd talked about such matters in principle when they were in Hamburg, in the mosque and in the flat.

What about the others?

Amir said simply there are no others. The others exist only to the degree that they fill the role we have designed for them. This is their function as others. Those who will die have no claim to their lives outside the useful fact of their dying.

Hammad was impressed by this. It sounded like philosophy.

Two women rustling through a park in the evening, in long skirts, one of them barefoot. Hammad sat on a bench, alone, watching, then got up and followed. This was something that just happened, the way a man is pulled out of his skin and then the body catches up. He followed only to the street where the park ended, watching as they disappeared, brief as turning pages.

The windshield is birdproof. The aileron is a movable flap.

He prays and sleeps, prays and eats. These are dumb junk meals often taken in silence. The plot shapes every breath he takes. This is the truth he has always looked for without knowing how to name it or where to search. They are together. There is no word they can speak, he and the others, that does not come back to this.

One of them peels an orange and begins to pick it apart.

You think too much, Hammad.

Men spent years organizing secretly this work.

Yes, okay.

I saw, myself, these men walking through the camp when we are there.

Okay. But the thinking is done.

And the talking.

Okay. Now we do it.

He hands a slice of orange over to Hammad, who is driving.

My father, the other man says, he would die three hundred times to know what we are doing.

We die once.

We die once, big-time.

Hammad thinks of the rapture of live explosives pressed to his chest and waist.

But don't forget, we are being stopped any minute by the CIA, the other man says.

He says this and then he laughs. Maybe it's not true anymore. Maybe it's a story they've told themselves so many times that they've stopped believing it. Or maybe they didn't believe it then and only begin to believe it now, nearing the time. Hammad sees nothing funny in this, either way.

The people he looked at, they need to be ashamed of their attachment to life, walking their dogs. Think of it, dogs scraping at dirt, lawn sprinklers hissing. When he saw a storm bearing in from the gulf he wanted to spread his arms and walk right into it. These people, what they hold so precious we see as empty space. He didn't think about the purpose of their mission. All he saw was shock and death. There is no purpose, this is the purpose.

When he walks down the bright aisle he thinks a thousand times in one second about what is coming. Clean-shaven, on videotape, passing through the metal detector. The girl at the checkout rolls the soup can over the scanner and he thinks of something funny he can say, saying it internally first to get the word order right.

He looked past the mud-brick huts toward the mountains. Bomb vest and black hood. We are willing to die, they are not. This is our strength, to love death, to feel the claim of armed martyrdom. He stood with the others in the old Russian copper mine, an Afghan camp now, theirs, and they listened to the amplified voice calling across the plain.

The vest was blue nylon with crisscross straps. There were canisters of high explosive wired into the belt. There were slabs of plastique high on his chest. This was not the method he and his brothers would one day employ but it was the same vision of heaven and hell, revenge and devastation.

They stood and listened to the recorded announcement, calling them to prayer.

Now he sits in the barber chair, wearing the striped cape. The barber is a slight man with little to say. The radio plays news, weather, sports and traffic. Hammad does not listen. He is thinking again, looking past the face in the mirror, which is not his, and waiting for the day to come, clear skies, light winds, when there is nothing left to think about.

PART THREE

DAVID JANIAK

10

They walked the entire route, north for twenty blocks and then across town and finally down toward Union Square, a couple of miles in steam heat, with police in riot helmets and flak jackets, small children riding their parents' shoulders. They walked with five hundred thousand others, a bright swarm of people ranging sidewalk to sidewalk, banners and posters, printed shirts, coffins draped in black, a march against the war, the president, the policies.

She felt remote from the occasion even as it pressed upon her. Police helicopters went beating overhead and there was a rank of men chanting and screaming at the marchers. Justin took a leaflet from a woman in a black headscarf. She had pigment dappled on her hands and looked off toward some middle distance, avoiding eye contact. People stopped to watch a burning float, papier-mâché, and the crowd became more dense, collapsing in on itself. She tried to take the kid's hand but that was over now. He was ten and thirsty and went dodging off to the other side of the street, where a man sold soft drinks from stacked crates. There were a dozen police nearby, positioned in front of red netting that was draped beneath a construction scaffold. This is where they would detain the overcommitted and uncontrollable.

A man came up to her, slouching out of the crowd, black man, hand on heart, and said, "This here's Charlie Parker's birthday."

He was almost looking at her but not quite and then moved on and said the same thing to a man wearing a T-shirt inscribed with a peace sign and in his reproachful tone she caught the implication that all these people, these half million in their running shoes and sun hats and symbol-bearing paraphernalia, were shit-faced fools to be gathered in this heat and humidity for whatever it was that had brought them here when they might more suitably be filling these streets, in exactly these numbers, to show respect to Charlie Parker on his birthday.

If her father were here, if Jack, he would probably agree. And, yes, she felt a separation, a distance. This crowd did not return to her a sense of belonging. She was here for the kid, to allow him to walk in the midst of dissent, to see and feel the argument against war and misrule. She wanted, herself, to be away from it all. These three years past, since that day in September, all life had become public. The stricken community pours forth voices and the solitary night mind is shaped by the outcry. She was content in the small guarded scheme she'd lately constructed, arranging the days, working the details, staying down, keeping out. Cut free from rage and foreboding. Cut free from nights that sprawl through endless waking chains of self-hell. She was marching apart from the handheld slogans and cardboard coffins, the mounted police, the anarchists throwing bottles. It was all choreography, to be shredded in seconds.

The kid turned and watched the man weave through the crowd, stopping here and there to make his announcement.

"Jazz musician," she told him. "Charlie Parker. Died forty or fifty years ago. When we get home I'll dig out some old long-playing records. LPs. Charlie Parker. Known as Bird. Don't ask me why. Before you ask, don't ask because I don't know. I'll find the records and we'll listen. But remind me. Because I forget."

The kid took more leaflets. People stood at the edges of the march handing out material on behalf of peace, justice, voter registration, paranoid truth movements. He studied the leaflets as he walked along, head bobbing so he could see the marchers in front of him, read the printed words in his hand.

Mourn the Dead. Heal the Wounded. End the War.

"Give yourself a break. Walk now, read later."

He said, "Yeah right."

"If you're trying to match what you read and what you see, they don't necessarily match."

He said, "Yeah right."

This was a new thing, the two drawled words of breezy dismissal. She pushed him toward the sidewalk and he drank his soda in the shade with his back against a building wall. She stood next to him, aware that he was slowly sinking down along the wall, a gestural comment on the heat and long walk, more drama than complaint.

Finally he came to rest in a tiny sumo squat. He sorted through his literature, spending some minutes looking at a particular leaflet. She saw the word *Islam* at the top of the middle page in the fold, followed by an 800 number. This was probably the leaflet he'd taken from the woman in the black headscarf. She saw words in boldface, with explanations.

A troupe of elderly women marched by singing an old protest song.

He said, "The Hajj."

"Yes."

He said, "The Shahadah."

"Yes."

"There is no god but Allah and Muhammad is His prophet."

"Yes."

He recited the line again, slowly, in a more concentrated manner, drawing it toward him in a way, trying to see into it. People stood nearby or shuffled past, marchers straying onto the sidewalk.

He recited the line in Arabic now. He recited the line, she told him it was Arabic, transliterated. But even this was too much, an isolated moment in the shade with her son, making her uneasy. He read the definition of another word that referred to the annual obligatory fast during the month of Ramadan. It made her think of something. He kept reading, mostly in silence and sometimes aloud, sticking the leaflet in the air and waiting for her to take it when he needed help pronouncing a word. This happened two or three times and when it didn't happen she found herself thinking of Cairo, some twenty years earlier, the vaguest shapes in her mind, herself among them, stepping off a tour bus into a vast crowd.

The trip was a gift, graduation, and she and a former classmate were on the bus and then off the bus and in the middle of some kind of festival. The crowd was large enough to make any part of it seem the middle. The crowd was dense and streaming, sundown, taking them along past booths and food stalls, and the friends were separated within half a minute. What she began to feel, aside from helplessness, was a heightened sense of who she was in relation to the others, thousands of them, orderly but all-enclosing. Those nearby saw her, smiled, some of them, and spoke to her, one or two, and she was forced to see herself in the reflecting surface of the crowd. She became whatever they sent back to her. She became her face and features, her skin color, a white person, white her fundamental meaning, her state of being. This is who she was, not really but at the same time yes, exactly, why not. She was privileged, detached, self-involved, white. It was there in her face, educated, unknowing, scared. She felt all the bitter truth that stereotypes contain. The crowd was gifted at being a crowd. This was their truth. They were at home, she thought, in the wave of bodies, the compressed mass. Being a crowd, this was a religion in itself, apart from the occasion they were there to celebrate. She thought of crowds in panic, surging over riverbanks. These were a white person's thoughts, the processing of white panic data. The others did not have these thoughts. Debra had these thoughts, her friend, her missing double, somewhere out there being white. She tried to look around for Debra but it was hard to do this, swing the shoulders free and turn. They were each in the middle of the crowd, they were the middle, each to herself. People talked to her. An old man offered her a sweet and told her the name of the festival, which marked the close of Ramadan. The memory ended here.

He recited the line in Arabic, by syllables, slowly, and she reached down for the leaflet and did her version, no less uncertain, only quicker. There were other words he handed up to her and she pronounced or mispronounced them and it made her uneasy, small as it was, reciting a line, explaining a ritual. It was part of the public discourse, the pouring forth, Islam with an 800 number. Even the old man's face, in memory, in Cairo, brought her back in. She was in that memory and on this sidewalk simultaneously, the ghost of one city, the frontal thunder of the other, and she needed to flee both crowds.

They rejoined the downtown stage of the march and listened briefly to someone speaking on a makeshift platform in Union Square. Then they went into the bookstore nearby and wandered the long aisles, in the cool and calm. Thousands of books, gleaming, on tables and shelves, the place quiet, a summer Sunday, and the kid went into a bloodhound imitation, looking and sniffing at books but not touching, his fingertips pressed to his face to create sagging jowls. She didn't know what this meant but began to understand that he wasn't trying to amuse her or annoy her. The behavior was outside her field of influence, between him and the books.

They rode the escalator to the second floor and spent some time looking at science books, nature books, foreign travel, *ficción*.

"What's the best thing you ever learned in school? Going back to the beginning, to the first days."

"The best thing."

"The biggest thing. Let's hear it, wise guy."

"You sound like Dad."

"I'm filling in. I'm doing double duty."

"When's he coming home?"

"Eight, nine days. What's the best thing?"

"The sun is a star."

"The best thing you ever learned."

"The sun is a star," he said.

"But didn't I teach you that?"

"I don't think so."

"You didn't learn that in school. I taught you that."

"I don't think so."

"We have a star map on our wall."

"The sun's not on our wall. It's out there. It's not *up* there. There is no up or down. It's just out there."

"Or maybe we're out here," she said. "That may be closer to the true state of things. We're the ones that are out somewhere."

They were enjoying this, a little tease and banter, and they stood at the tall window watching the end of the march, banners lowered and folded, the crowd splitting, drifting off, people moving toward the park or into the subway or the cross streets.

It was amazing in a way, what he'd said, one sentence, five words, and think of everything it says about everything there is. The sun is a star. When did she realize this herself and why didn't she remember when? The sun is a star. It seemed a revelation, a fresh way to think about being who we are, the purest way and only finally unfolding, a kind of mystical shiver, an awakening.

Maybe she was just tired. It was time to go home, eat something, drink something. Eight or nine days or longer. Buy the kid a book and go home.

That night she sorted through her father's collection of jazz records and played a side or two for Justin. After he'd gone to bed she thought of something else and took a jazz encyclopedia down from the dusty upper shelves and there it was, in six-point type, not only the year but the month and the day. This was Charlie Parker's birthday.

She counted down from one hundred by sevens. It made her feel good to do this. There were mishaps now and then. Odd numbers were tricky, like some rough tumble through space, resisting the easy run of what is divisible by two. That's why they wanted her to count down by sevens, to make it not so easy. She could descend into the single digits most times without a stumble. The most anxious transition was twenty-three to sixteen. She wanted to say seventeen. She was always on the verge of going from thirty-seven to thirty to twenty-three to seventeen. The odd number asserting itself. At the medical center the doctor smiled at the error, or didn't notice, or was looking at a printout of test results. She was troubled by memory lapses, steeped in family history. She was also fine. Brain normal for age. She was forty-one years old and within the limited protocols of the imaging process, pretty much everything seemed to be unremarkable. The ventricles were unremarkable, the brainstem and cerebellum, base of skull, cavernous sinus regions, pituitary gland. All unremarkable.

She took the tests and examination, did the MRI, did the psychometrics, did word pairing, recall, concentration, walked a straight line wall to wall, counted down from one hundred by sevens.

It made her feel good, the counting down, and she did it sometimes in the day's familiar drift, walking down a street, riding in a taxi. It was her form of lyric verse, subjective and unrhymed, a little songlike but with a rigor, a tradition of fixed order, only backwards, to test the presence of another kind of reversal, which a doctor nicely named retrogenesis.

At the Race & Sports Book, downtown, in the old casino, there were five rows of long tables set at graded levels. He sat at the far end of the last table in the top row, facing front, with five screens high on the wall ahead showing horses running in various time zones somewhere on the planet. A man read a paperback book at the table directly below him, cigarette burning down in his hand. Across the room at the lowest level a large woman in a hooded sweatshirt sat before an array of newspapers. He knew it was a woman because the hood was not raised and would have known anyway, somehow, through gesture or posture, the way she spread pages before her and used both hands to smooth them out and then nudged other pages out of reading range, in the wan light and hanging smoke.

The casino spread behind him and to either side, acres of neon slots, mostly empty now of human pulse. He felt hemmed in all the same, enclosed by the dimness and low ceiling and by the thick residue of smoke that adhered to his skin and carried decades of crowds and action.

It was eight a.m. and he was the only person who knew this. He glanced toward the far end of the adjacent table, where an old man with a white ponytail sat bent across the arm of his chair, watching horses in midrace and showing the anxious lean of body english that marks money on the line. He was otherwise motionless. The lean was all there was and then the voice of the track announcer, rapid-fire, the one mild excitement: *Yankee Gal coming through on the inside.*

There was no one else at the tables here. Races ended, others began, or they were the same races replayed on one or more of the screens. He wasn't watching closely. There were flutters of action from another set of screens, recessed at a lower level, above the cashier's cage. He watched the cigarette burn down in the hand of the man reading the book, just below him. He checked his watch again. He knew time and day of week and wondered when such scraps of data would begin to feel disposable.

The ponytailed man got up and left in the final furlong of a race in progress, curling his newspaper into a tight fold and snapping it on his thigh. The whole place stank of abandonment. In time Keith got up and walked over to the poker room, where he completed his buy-in and took his seat, ready for the start of the tournament, so-called.

Only three tables were occupied. In about the seventy-seventh game of hold 'em, he began to sense a life in all this, not for himself but the others, a small dawn of tunneled meaning. He watched the blinking woman across the table. She was thin, wrinkled, hard to see, right there, five feet away, hair going gray. He didn't wonder who she was or where she'd go when this was over, to what sort of room somewhere, to think what kind of thoughts. This was never over. That was the point. There was nothing outside the game but faded space. She blinked and called, blinked and folded.

In the casino distance, the announcer's smoky voice, in replay. Yankee Gal was coming through on the inside.

She missed those nights with friends when you talk about everything. She hadn't stayed in close touch and felt no guilt or need. There were hours of talk and laughter, bottles uncorked. She missed the comical midlife monologues of the clinically self-absorbed. The food ran out, the wine did not, and who was the little man in the red cravat who did sound effects from old submarine movies. She went out only rarely now, went alone, did not stay late. She missed the autumn weekends at somebody's country house, leaf-fall and touch football, kids tumbling down grassy slopes, leaders and followers, all watched by a pair of tall slender dogs poised on their haunches like figures in myth.

She didn't feel the old attraction, the thing looked forward to. It was also a question of thinking of Keith. He would not want to do it. He'd never felt right in these surroundings and it would be impossible now for him to feel any different. People have trouble approaching him on the simplest social level. They think they will bounce off. They will hit a wall and bounce.

Her mother, this is what she missed. Nina was all around her now but only in the meditative air, her face and breath, an attending presence somewhere near.

After the memorial service, four months earlier, a small group went for a late lunch. Martin had flown in from somewhere, as usual, in Europe, and there were two of her mother's former colleagues.

It was a quiet hour and a half, with stories of Nina and other matters, the work they were doing, the places they'd lately been. The woman, a biographer, ate sparingly, spoke at some length. The man said nearly nothing. He was director of a library of art and architecture.

The afternoon was fading away, over coffee. Then Martin said, "We're all sick of America and Americans. The subject nauseates us."

He and Nina had seen each other only rarely in the last two and a half years of her life. Each heard news of the other through mutual friends or from Lianne, who stayed in touch with Martin, sporadically, through e-mails and phone calls.

"But I'll tell you something," he said.

She looked at him. He had the same thirteen-day beard, the drooping lids of chronic jet lag. He wore the standard unpressed suit, his uniform, shirt looking slept-in, no tie. Someone displaced or deeply distracted, lost in time. But he was heavier now, his face went east and west, there were signs of bloat and sag that the beard could not conceal. He had the pressured look of a man whose eyes have gone smaller in his head.

"For all the careless power of this country, let me say this, for all the danger it makes in the world, America is going to become irrelevant. Do you believe this?"

She wasn't sure why she'd stayed in touch with him. The disincentives were strong. There was what she knew about him, even if incomplete, and there was, more tellingly, how her mother had come to feel about him. It was guilt by association, his, when the towers fell.

"There is a word in German. *Gedankenübertragung*. This is the broadcasting of thoughts. We are all beginning to have this thought, of American irrelevance. It's a little like telepathy. Soon the day is coming when nobody has to think about America except for the danger it brings. It is losing the center. It becomes the center of its own shit. This is the only center it occupies."

She wasn't sure what had brought this on, maybe something

that someone had said, passingly, at an earlier point. Maybe Martin was having an argument with the dead, with Nina. They were clearly wishing they'd gone home, the colleagues, before the coffee and biscuits. This was not the occasion, the woman said, to argue global politics. Nina could have done it better than any of us, she said, but Nina isn't here and the talk dishonors her memory.

Martin waved a hand in dismissal, rejecting the narrow terms of discourse. He was a link to her mother, Lianne thought. That's why she'd stayed in touch. Even when her mother was alive, fadingly, he helped Lianne think of her in clearer outline. Ten or fifteen minutes on the phone with him, a man etched in regret but also love and reminiscence, or longer conversations that wandered toward an hour, and she'd feel both sadder and better, seeing Nina in a kind of freeze-frame, vivid and alert. She'd tell her mother about these calls and watch her face, looking hard for a sign of light.

Now she watched him.

The colleagues insisted on picking up the check. Martin did not contest the matter. He was done with them. They embodied a form of cautionary tact better left to state funerals in autocratic countries. Before leaving, the library director took a sunflower from the bud vase at the center of the table and placed it in the breast pocket of Martin's jacket. He did this with a smile, possibly hostile, maybe not. Then he finally spoke, standing over the table and fitting his long body into a raincoat.

"If we occupy the center, it's because you put us there. This is your true dilemma," he said. "Despite everything, we're still America, you're still Europe. You go to our movies, read our books, listen to our music, speak our language. How can you stop thinking about us? You see us and hear us all the time. Ask yourself. What comes after America?"

Martin spoke quietly, almost idly, to himself.

"I don't know this America anymore. I don't recognize it," he said. "There's an empty space where America used to be."

They stayed, she and Martin, the only patrons left in the long room, below street level, and talked for some time. She told him about the last hard months of her mother's life, ruptured blood vessels, loss of muscle control, the smeared speech and empty gaze. He bent low over the table, breathing audibly. She wanted to hear him talk about Nina and he did. It seemed all she'd known of her mother for an extended time was Nina in a chair, Nina in a bed. He lifted her into artists' lofts, Byzantine ruins, into halls where she'd lectured, Barcelona to Tokyo.

"I used to imagine, when I was a girl, that I was her. I stood sometimes in the middle of the room and spoke to a chair or sofa. I said very smart things about painters. I knew how to pronounce every name, all the hard names, and I knew their paintings from books and museum visits."

"You were frequently alone."

"I couldn't understand why my mother and father split up. My mother never cooked. My father never seemed to eat. What could go wrong?"

"You will always be a daughter, I think. First and always, this is what you are."

"And you are always what?"

"I am always your mother's lover. Long before I knew her. Always that. It was waiting to happen."

"You almost make me believe it."

The other thing she wanted to believe was that his physical bearing was not evidence of illness or some steep financial setback affecting his morale. It was the end of the long story, he and Nina, that had brought him to this dispirited point. Nothing more or less than that. This is what she believed and this is what stirred her sympathy.

"Some people are lucky. They become who they are supposed to be," he said. "This did not happen to me until I met
your mother. One day we started to talk and it never stopped,
this conversation."

"Even at the end of things."

"Even when we no longer found agreeable things to say or
anything at all to say. The conversation never ended."

"I believe you."

"From the first day."

"In Italy," she said.

"Yes. This is true."

"And the second day. In front of a church," she said. "The
two of you. And someone took your picture."

He looked up and seemed to study her, wondering what
else she knew. She would not tell him what she knew or that
she'd made no effort to find out more. She had not gone to
libraries to examine the histories of underground movements in
those years and she had not searched the Internet for traces of
the man called Ernst Hechinger. Her mother hadn't, she hadn't.

"There's a plane to catch."

"What would you do without your planes?"

"There's always a plane to catch."

"Where would you be?" she said. "One city, which one?"

He'd come for the day, without a suitcase or carry-on. He'd
sold his New York apartment and had reduced the number of his
commitments here.

"I don't think I'm ready to face that question. One city," he
said, "and I am trapped."

They knew him here and the waiter brought complimentary
brandies. They lingered a while longer, into twilight. She realized
she would never see him again.

She'd respected his secret, yielded to his mystery. Whatever it was he'd done, it was not outside the lines of response. She could imagine his life, then and now, detect the slurred pulse of an earlier consciousness. Maybe he was a terrorist but he was one of ours, she thought, and the thought chilled her, shamed her— one of ours, which meant godless, Western, white.

He stood and lifted the flower out of his breast pocket. Then he smelled it and tossed it on the table, smiling at her. They touched hands briefly and went out to the street, where she watched him walk to the corner, arm raised to the tide of passing cabs.

11

The dealer touched the green button, a fresh deck rose to the tabletop.

In these months of mastering the game he was spending most of his time on the Strip now, sitting in leather recliners in the sports-book parlors, hunched under shade canopies in the poker rooms. He was finally making money, quiet amounts that began to show consistency. He was also going home periodically, three or four days, love, sex, fatherhood, home-cooked food, but was lost at times for something to say. There was no language, it seemed, to tell them how he spent his days and nights.

Soon he felt the need to be back there. When his plane came down over the desert he could easily believe that this was a place he'd always known. There were standard methods and routines. Taxi to the casino, taxi back to his hotel. He managed on two meals a day, didn't require more. The heat pressed into metal and glass, made the streets seem to shimmer. At the table he didn't study players for tells, didn't care why they coughed or seemed bored or scratched a forearm. He studied the cards and knew the tendencies. There was that and the blinking woman. He remembered her from the casino downtown, invisible except for the fretful eyes. The blinking was not a tell. It was only who she was, some grown man's mother firing chips into the pot, blinking in nature's own arrangement, like a firefly in a field. He drank hard liquor sparingly, nearly not at all, and allowed himself five hours' sleep, barely aware of setting limits and restrictions. Never occurred to him to light up a cigar, as in the old days, at the old game. He walked through crowded hotel lobbies under hand-painted Sistine ceilings and into the high glare of this or that casino, not looking at people, seeing essentially no one, but every time he boarded a flight he glanced at faces on both sides of the aisle, trying to spot the man or men who might be a danger to them all.

When it happened he wondered why he hadn't known it would. It happened in one of the high-caste casinos, five hundred players assembled for a no-limit hold 'em tournament with a major buy-in. Over there, at the other end of the room, above the heads at the clustered tables, a man was standing to do a series of flexing exercises, loosen the neck and shoulder muscles, get the blood running. There was an element of pure ritual in his movements, something beyond the functional. He took deep full abdominal breaths, then dipped a hand toward the table and appeared to toss some chips into the pot without glancing at the action that spurred the bet. The man was strangely familiar. What was strange is this, that after the passage of several years someone might look so very different while being unequivocally himself. It had to be Terry Cheng, easing back into his chair now, dropping out of Keith's line of vision, and of course this is who it was because how could any of this be happening, the poker circuit, the thunderous runs of money, the comped hotel rooms and high competition, without the presence of Terry Cheng.

It wasn't until the next day, when the woman at the podium was making announcements about available seats at certain tables, that they stood together outside the rail.

Terry Cheng showed a wan smile. He wore tinted glasses and an olive jacket with wide lapels and glossy buttons. The jacket was too large, hanging off his shoulders. He wore loose trousers and hotel slippers, velour, and a silk shirt gone stale with wear.

Keith half expected him to speak in fifth-century Mandarin.

"I was wondering how long it would take you to spot me."

"You spotted me, I take it."

"About a week ago," Terry said.

"And said nothing."

"You were deep in your game. What would I say? Next time I looked up, you weren't there."

"I go to the sports book to relax. Eat a sandwich and drink a beer. I like the action going on around me, all the screens, all the sports. I drink a beer and pretty much ignore it."

"I like to sit by the waterfall. I order a mild drink. Ten thousand people around me. In the aisles, in the aquarium, in the garden, at the slots. I sip a mild drink."

Terry seemed to lean left, like a man about to drift toward an exit. He'd lost weight and looked older and spoke in an unfamiliar voice with a scratchy edge.

"You're staying here."

"When I'm in town. Rooms are high and wide," Terry said. "One wall is all window."

"Costs you nothing."

"Incidentals."

"A serious player."

"I'm in their computer. Everything's in their computer. Everything's entered. If you lift an item from the minibar and don't return it inside sixty seconds it's charged directly and instantaneously to your account."

He liked this, Terry did. Keith was undecided.

"When you check in, they give you a map. I still need it,

after all this time. I never know where I am. Room service brings tea bags in the shape of pyramids. Everything's very dimensional. I tell them not to bring me a newspaper. If you don't read a newspaper, you're never a day behind."

They talked a minute longer, then went to their designated tables without making plans to meet later. The idea of later was elusive.

The kid stood at the far end of the table, spreading mustard on bread. She saw no trace of other forms of food.

She said, "I used to have a decent pen. Sort of silverish. Maybe you've seen it."

He stopped and thought, eyes narrow, face going glassy. This meant he'd seen the pen, used it, lost it, given it away or traded it for something stupid.

"We have no serious writing instruments in this house."

She knew what this sounded like.

"You have a hundred pencils and we have a dozen bad ball-point pens."

It sounded like the decline and fall of literate exchange on a surface such as paper. She watched him dip the knife back in the jar and spread the mustard carefully along the borders of the slice of bread.

"What's wrong with ballpoints?" he said.

"They're bad."

"What's bad about a pencil?"

"All right, pencils. Wood and lead. Pencils are serious. Wood and graphite. Materials from the earth. We respect this about a pencil."

"Where's he going this time?"

"Paris. Major competition. I may join him for a few days."

He stopped and thought again.

"What happens to me?"

"You live your life. Just be sure to lock the door behind you when you get home after a night of drinking and carousing."

"Yeah right."

"Do you know what carousing is?"

"Sort of."

"Me too. Sort of," she said. "And I'm not going anywhere."

"Don't you think I know that?"

She stood at the window watching him fold the bread and take a bite. This was whole-grain bread, nine-grain, ten-grain, no trans fat, good source of fiber. She didn't know what the mustard was.

"What did you do with the pen? Silver pen. You know what I'm talking about."

"I think he took it."

"You think what. No, he didn't. He doesn't need a pen."

"He needs to write things. Just like anybody."

"He didn't take it."

"I'm not blaming him. I'm just saying."

"Not this pen. He didn't take this pen. So where is it?"

He looked into the tabletop.

"I think he took it. He might not even know he took it. I'm not blaming him."

He was still standing, bread in hand, and would not look at her. He said, "I really, honestly think he took it."

People everywhere, many with cameras.

"You've burnished your game," Terry said.

"Something like that."

"The situation is going to change. All the attention, the television coverage, the armies of recruits, all soon to fade."

"That's good."

"That's good," Terry said.

"We'll still be here."

"We're poker players," he said.

They sat in the lounge near the waterfall with soft drinks and snacks. Terry Cheng wore the hotel slippers, no socks, and ignored the cigarette that burned in his ashtray.

"There's an underground game, private game, high stakes, select cities. It's like a forbidden religion springing up again. Five-card stud and draw."

"Our old game."

"There are two games. Phoenix and Dallas. What's that part of Dallas? Well-to-do."

"Highland Park."

"Well-to-do people, older people, leaders of the community. Know the game, respect the game."

"Five-card stud."

"Stud and draw."

"You do well. You win big," Keith said.

"I own their souls," Terry said.

Crowds moved around the open lounge, which vaguely resembled a carousel, hotel guests, gamblers, tourists, people headed to the restaurants, the lush shops, the art gallery.

"Did you smoke back then, when we played?"

"I don't know. Tell me," Terry said.

"I think you were the only one who didn't smoke. We had a number of cigars and one cigarette. But I don't think it was you."

There were isolated instants, now and then, sitting here, when Terry Cheng seemed again to be the man at the table in

Keith's apartment, dividing chips in swift and artful fashion
after the high-low games. He was one of them, only better at
cards, and not really one of them at all.

"Did you see the man at my table?"

"In the surgical mask."

"Significant winner," Terry said.

"I can picture it spreading."

"The mask, yes."

"Three or four people one day, showing up in surgical
masks."

"No one knows why."

"Then there are ten more and then ten more after that.
Like those bicycle riders in China."

"Whatever," Terry said. "Exactly."

Each followed the other's line of thought along the narrowest track. Around them a wordless din so deeply settled in
the air and walls and furniture, in the moving bodies of men and
women that it wasn't easily separable from no sound at all.

"It's a break from the circuit. They drink aged bourbon and
have wives in the other rooms somewhere."

"Dallas, you're saying."

"Yes."

"I don't know."

"There's a game getting started in Los Angeles. Same thing,
stud and draw. Younger crowd. Like early Christians in hiding.
Think about it."

"I don't know. I'm not sure I could survive a couple of nights
in that kind of social arrangement."

"I think it was Rumsey. The one man," Terry said, "who
smoked cigarettes."

Keith stared into the waterfall, forty yards away. He realized
he didn't know whether it was real or simulated. The flow was

unruffled and the sound of falling water might easily be a digital effect like the waterfall itself.

He said, "Rumsey was cigars."

"Rumsey was cigars. You're probably right."

For all his looseness of manner, the clothing that didn't fit, the tendency to get lost in the hotel's deeper reaches and outlying promenades, Terry was set inflexibly in this life. There was no rule of correspondence here. This was not balanced by that. There was no element that might be seen in the light of another element. It was all one thing, whatever the venue, the city, the prize money. Keith saw the point of this. He preferred this to private games with easy banter and wives arranging flowers, a format that appealed to Terry's vanity, he thought, but could not match the crucial anonymity of these days and weeks, the mingling of countless lives that had no stories attached.

"Did you ever look at that waterfall? Are you able to convince yourself you're looking at water, real water, and not some special effect?"

"I don't think about it. It's not something we're supposed to think about," Terry said.

His cigarette had burned down to the filter.

"I worked in midtown. I didn't experience the impact that others felt, down there, where you were," he said. "I'm told, someone told me that Rumsey's mother. What is it now? She took a shoe. She took one of his shoes and she took a razor blade. She went to his apartment and got these things, whatever she could find that might contain genetic material, like traces of hair or skin. There was an armory where she took these things for a DNA match."

Keith stared into the waterfall.

"She went back a day or two later. Who told me this? She took something else, I don't know, a toothbrush. Then she went

204

back again. She took something else. Then she went back again. Then they moved the location. That's when she stopped going."

Terry Cheng, the old Terry, had never been so talkative. Telling even a brief story was outside the limits of what he took to be a superior self-restraint.

"I used to tell people. People talked about where they were, where they worked. I said midtown. The word sounded naked. It sounded neutral, like it was nowhere. I heard he went out a window, Rumsey."

Keith looked into the waterfall. This was better than closing his eyes. If he closed his eyes, he'd see something.

"You went back to work in the law office for a while. I remember we talked."

"It was a different firm and not a law office."

"Whatever," Terry said.

"That's what it was, whatever."

"But here we are and here we'll be when the craze dies down."

"You still play online."

"I do, yes, but I can't give this up. Here we'll be."

"And the man in the surgical mask."

"Yes, he'll be here."

"And the blinking woman."

"I haven't seen the blinking woman," Terry said.

"One day I'll speak to her."

"You've seen the dwarf."

"Once only. Then he was gone."

"A dwarf named Carlo. Significant loser. He's the only player whose name I know except for you. I know the name because it belongs to a dwarf. There's no other reason to know it."

The massed slots bubbled behind them.

_____

When he heard the news on the radio, School Number One, many children, he knew he had to call her. Terrorists taking hostages, the siege, the explosions, this was Russia, somewhere, hundreds dead, many children.

She spoke quietly.

"They had to know. They made a situation that had to come to this, with children. They absolutely had to know. They went there to die. They made a situation, with children, specifically, and they knew how it would end. They had to know."

There was silence at either end. After a time she said it was warm, in the eighties, and added that the kid was fine, the kid was all right. There was an edge in her voice, followed by another silence. He tried to listen into this, find the link in her remarks. In the deep pause he began to see himself standing exactly where he was, in a room somewhere, in a hotel somewhere, with a telephone in his hand.

She told him that the findings were unremarkable. There was no sign of impairment. She kept using the word *unremarkable*. She loved the word. The word expressed enormous relief. There were no lesions, hemorrhages or infarcts. She read the results to him and he stood in his room and listened. There was so much to report that was unremarkable. She loved the word *infarct*. Then she said she wasn't sure she believed the findings. Okay for now but what about later? He'd told her many times and told her again that she was devising ways to be afraid. This wasn't fear, she said, but only skepticism. She was doing well. She had normal morphology, she said, quoting the report. She loved this term but couldn't quite believe it referred to her. It was a question of skepticism, she said, from the Greek for skeptic. Then she talked about her father. She was slightly drunk, not half smashed but maybe a quarter, which was about as smashed as she ever got. She talked about her father and asked about his. Then she laughed and said, "Listen," and she began to recite a series of numbers, pausing a beat between each, using a happy sort of singsong.

One hundred, ninety-three, eighty-six, seventy-nine.

He missed the kid. Neither liked talking on the phone. How do you talk to a kid on the phone? He talked to her. They talked sometimes in the middle of the night, her time, or middle of the night, his time. She described her position in bed, curled up, hand between her legs, or body spread wide above the sheets, phone on the pillow, and he heard her murmuring in the double distance, hand to breast, hand to pussy, seeing her so clearly he thought his head might explode.

12

There was a show of Morandi paintings at a gallery in Chelsea, still lifes, six of them, and a couple of drawings, still lifes, and of course she went. She had mixed feelings about going but went. Because even this, bottles and jars, a vase, a glass, simple shapes in oil on canvas, pencil on paper, brought her back into the midst of it, the thrust of arguments, perceptions, deadly politics, her mother and her mother's lover.

Nina had insisted on returning the two paintings on her living room wall. They went back to Martin in the early stages of their estrangement, and the old passport photos as well. This was work done half a century earlier, the paintings, and the photographs were much older, most of them, and it was work that both women loved. But she honored her mother's wishes, arranged the shipment, thought of the dollar value of the paintings, respected her mother's integrity, thought of the paintings themselves, Berlin-bound, to be bargained over and sold in a cell-phone transaction. The room was tomblike without them.

The gallery was in an old industrial building with a cage elevator that required a living human, full-time, to crank the lever on a rotary control, bouncing visitors up and down the shaft.

She went down a long dim corridor and found the gallery.

There was no one there. She stood at the first canvas, looking. The show was small, the paintings were small. She stepped back, moved close. She liked this, alone in a room, looking.

She looked at the third painting for a long time. It was a variation on one of the paintings her mother had owned. She noted the nature and shape of each object, the placement of objects, the tall dark oblongs, the white bottle. She could not stop looking. There was something hidden in the painting. Nina's living room was there, memory and motion. The objects in the painting faded into the figures behind them, the woman smoking in the chair, the standing man. In time she moved on to the next painting and the next, fixing each in her mind, and then there were the drawings. She hadn't approached the drawings yet.

A man came in. He was interested in looking at her before he looked at the paintings. Maybe he expected certain freedoms to be in effect because they were like-minded people in a run-down building, here to look at art.

She moved through the open doorway into the office area, where the drawings hung. At the desk a young man leaned over a laptop. She examined the drawings. She wasn't sure why she was looking so intently. She was passing beyond pleasure into some kind of assimilation. She was trying to absorb what she saw, take it home, wrap it around her, sleep in it. There was so much to see. Turn it into living tissue, who you are.

She went back to the main room but could not look at the work the same way with the man there, watching her or not. He wasn't watching her but he was there, fifty and leathery, a mug-shot monochrome, probably a painter, and she went out of the room and down the corridor, where she hit the elevator button.

She realized she hadn't picked up a catalog but didn't go back. She didn't need a catalog. The elevator came rattling up the shaft. Nothing detached in this work, nothing free of personal resonance. All the paintings and drawings carried the same title. *Natura Morta*. Even this, the term for still life, yielded her mother's last days.

There were times, in the sports book, when he glanced at one of the screens and wasn't sure whether he was seeing a fragment of live action or of slow-motion replay. It was a lapse that should have unsettled him, an issue of basic brain function, one reality versus another, but it all seemed a matter of false distinctions, fast, slow, now, then, and he drank his beer and listened to the mingled sounds.

He never bet on these events. It was the effect on the senses that drew him here. Everything happened remotely, even the nearest noise. The high room was dimly lit, men seated heads up, or standing, or walking through, and out of the stealthy tension in the air come the shouts, a horse breaking out of the pack, a runner rounding second, and the action moves to the foreground, there to here, life or death. He liked listening to the visceral burst, men on their feet, calling out, a rough salvo of voices that brought heat and open emotion to the soft pall of the room. Then it was over, gone in seconds, and he liked that too.

He showed his money in the poker room. The cards fell randomly, no assignable cause, but he remained the agent of free choice. Luck, chance, no one knew what these things were. These things were only assumed to affect events. He had memory, judgment, the ability to decide what is true, what is alleged, when to strike, when to fade. He had a measure of calm, of calculated isolation, and there was a certain logic he might draw on. Terry Cheng said that the only true logic in the game was the logic of personality. But the game had structure, guiding principles, sweet and easy interludes of dream logic when the player

211

knows that the card he needs is the card that's sure to fall. Then, always, in the crucial instant ever repeated hand after hand, the choice of yes or no. Call or raise, call or fold, the little binary pulse located behind the eyes, the choice that reminds you who you are. It belonged to him, this yes or no, not to a horse running in the mud somewhere in New Jersey.

She lived in the spirit of what is ever impending.

They embraced, saying nothing. Later they spoke in low tones that carried a nuance of tact. They would share nearly four full days of indirection before they talked about things that mattered. It was lost time, designed from the first hour to go unremembered. She would remember the song. They spent nights in bed with the windows open, traffic noises, voices carrying, five or six girls marching down the street at two a.m. singing an old rock ballad that she sang along with them, softly, lovingly, word for word, matching accents, pauses and breaks, hating to hear the voices fade. Words, their own, were not much more than sounds, airstreams of shapeless breath, bodies speaking. There was a breeze if they were lucky but even in the damp heat on the top floor under a tar roof she kept the air conditioner off. He needed to feel real air, she said, in a real room, with thunder rumbling just above.

On these nights it seemed to her that they were falling out of the world. This was not a form of erotic illusion. She was continuing to withdraw, but calmly, in control. He was self-sequestered, as always, but with a spatial measure now, one of air miles and cities, a dimension of literal distance between himself and others.

They took the kid to a couple of museums and then she watched them toss a baseball in the park. Justin threw hard. He wasted no time. He snatched the ball out of the air, took it in his bare hand, smacked it back into the glove, reared back and threw hard and then, next toss, maybe a little harder. He was like a pitching machine with hair and teeth, register set to peak velocity. Keith was amused, then impressed, then puzzled. He told the kid to calm down, ease up. He told him to follow through. There was the windup, the release, the follow-through. He told him he was burning a hole in his old man's hand.

She came across a poker tournament on TV. He was in the next room scanning a landfill of accumulated mail. She saw three or four tables, in long shot, with spectators seated among them, clustered in pockets, in spooky blue light. The tables were slightly elevated, players immersed in a fluorescent glow and bent in mortal tension. She didn't know where this was taking place, or when, and she didn't know why the usual method was not in effect, close-ups of thumbs, knuckles, cards and faces. But she watched. She hit the mute button and looked at the players seated around the tables as the camera slowly swept the room and she realized that she was waiting to see Keith. The spectators sat in that icy violet light, able to see little or nothing. She wanted to see her husband. The camera caught the faces of players previously obscured and she looked closely, one by one. She imagined herself in cartoon format, a total fool, hurrying to Justin's room, hair flying, and dragging him out of bed and standing him up in front of the screen so he could see his father, *Look*, in Rio or London or Las Vegas. His father was twenty feet away at the desk in the next room reading bank statements and writing checks. She watched a while longer, looking for him, and then she stopped.

They talked on day four, sitting in the living room, late, with a horsefly fixed to the ceiling.

"There are things I understand."

"All right."

"I understand there are some men who are only half here.

213

Let's not say men. Let's say people. People who are more or less obscure at times."

"You understand this."

"They protect themselves this way, themselves and others. I understand this. But then there's the other thing and that's the family. This is the point I want to make, that we need to stay together, keep the family going. Just us, three of us, long-term, under the same roof, not every day of the year or every month but with the idea that we're permanent. Times like these, the family is necessary. Don't you think? Be together, stay together? This is how we live through the things that scare us half to death."

"All right."

"We need each other. Just people sharing the air, that's all."

"All right," he said.

"But I know what's happening. You're going to drift away. I'm prepared for that. You'll stay away longer, drift off somewhere. I know what you want. It's not exactly a wish to disappear. It's the thing that leads to that. Disappearing is the consequence. Or maybe it's the punishment."

"You know what I want. I don't know. You know."

"You want to kill somebody," she said.

She didn't look at him when she said this.

"You've wanted this for some time," she said. "I don't know how it works or how it feels. But it's a thing you carry with you."

Now that she'd said it, she wasn't sure she believed it. But she was certain he'd never argued the idea in his mind. It was in his skin, maybe just a pulse at the side of the forehead, the faintest cadence in a small blue vein. She knew there was something that had to be satisfied, a matter discharged in full, and she thought this was at the heart of his restlessness.

"Too bad I can't join the army. Too old," he said, "or I could kill without penalty and then come home and be a family."

He was drinking scotch, sipping it, neat, and smiling faintly at what he'd said.

"You can't go back to the job you had. I understand that."

"The job. The job wasn't much different from the job I had before all this happened. But that was before, this is after."

"I know that most lives make no sense. I mean in this country, what makes sense? I can't sit here and say let's go away for a month. I'm not going to reduce myself to saying something like that. Because that's another world, the one that makes sense. But listen to me. You were stronger than I was. You helped me get here. I don't know what would have happened."

"I can't talk about strength. What strength?"

"That's what I saw and felt. You were the one in the tower but I was the berserk. Now, damn it, I don't know."

After a silence he said, "I don't know either," and they laughed.

"I used to watch you sleep. I know how strange that sounds. But it wasn't strange. Just by being who you were, being alive and back here with us. I watched you. I felt I knew you in a way I'd never known you before. We were a family. That's what it was. That's how we did it."

"Look, trust me."

"All right."

"I'm not set on doing anything permanent," he said. "I go away a while, come back. I'm not about to disappear. Not about to do anything drastic. I'm here now and I'll be back. You want me back. Is that right?"

"Yes."

"Go away, come back. Simple as that."

"There's money coming," she said. "The sale is almost complete."

"Money coming."

"Yes," she said.

He'd helped work out details of the transaction concerning her mother's apartment. He'd read contracts, made adjustments and e-mailed instructions from a casino on some Indian reservation where a tournament was in progress.

"Money coming," he said again. "The kid's education. Now through college, eleven or twelve years, criminal sums of money. But that's not what you're saying. You're saying we can afford a major loss I might suffer in the card rooms. This won't happen."

"If you believe it, I believe it."

"Hasn't happened and it won't," he said.

"What about Paris? Will that happen?"

"It became Atlantic City. A month from now."

"How does the warden feel about conjugal visits?"

"You don't want to be there."

"I don't. You're right," she said. "Because thinking about it is one thing. Seeing it would put me in depression. People sitting around a table going shuffle shuffle. Week after week. I mean catching planes to go play cards. I mean aside from the absurdity, the total psychotic folly, isn't there something very sad about this?"

"You said it yourself. Most lives make no sense."

"But isn't it demoralizing? Doesn't it wear you down? It must eat away your spirit. I mean I was watching on TV last night. Like a séance in hell. Tick tock tick tock. What happens after months of this? Or years. Who do you become?"

He looked at her and nodded as if he agreed and then kept nodding, taking the gesture to another level, a kind of deep sleep, a narcolepsy, eyes open, mind shut down.

There was one final thing, too self-evident to need saying. She wanted to be safe in the world and he did not.

13

When she received a summons for jury service some months earlier and reported to the United States District Court with five hundred other potential jurors and learned that the trial for which they'd been assembled concerned a lawyer accused of aiding the cause of terrorism, she filled out the forty-five-page questionnaire with truths, half-truths and heartfelt lies.

For some time before that day she'd been offered books to edit on terrorism and related subjects. Every subject seemed related. She wasn't sure why she'd been so desperate to work on such books during the weeks and months when she could not sleep and there were songs of desert mystics in the hallway.

The trial was now in progress but she didn't follow it in the newspaper. She'd been Juror Number 121, excused from serving on the basis of her written responses. She didn't know whether it was the true answers or the lies that had made this happen.

She knew that the lawyer, an American woman, was associated with a radical Muslim cleric who was serving a life sentence for terrorist activity. She knew that the man was blind. This was common knowledge. He was the Blind Sheik. But she didn't know the details of the charges made against the lawyer because she wasn't reading the stories in the newspaper.

She was editing a book on early polar exploration and another on late Renaissance art and she was counting down from one hundred by sevens.

Died by his own hand.

For nineteen years, since he fired the shot that killed him, she'd said these words to herself periodically, in memoriam, beautiful words that had an archaic grain, Middle English, Old Norse. She imagined the words engraved on an old slant tombstone in a neglected churchyard somewhere in New England.

The grandparents hold sacred office. They're the ones with the deepest memories. But the grandparents are nearly all gone. Justin has only one now, his father's father, disinclined to travel, a man whose memories have settled into the tight circuit of his days, beyond easy radius of the child. The child is yet to grow into the deep shadow of his own memories. She herself, mother-daughter, is somewhere midway in the series, knowing that one memory at least is inescapably secure, the day that has marked her awareness of who she is and how she lives.

Her father wasn't buried in a windy churchyard under bare trees. Jack was in a marble vault high on a wall in a mausoleum complex outside Boston with several hundred others, all chambered in tiers, floor to ceiling.

She came across the obituary late one night, looking at a newspaper that was six days old.

They die every day, Keith said once. There's no news in that.

He was back in Las Vegas now and she was in bed, flipping the pages, reading the obits. The force of this obituary did not register at once. A man named David Janiak, 39. The account of his life and death was brief and sketchy, written in haste to make a deadline, she thought. She thought there would be a complete report in the paper of the following day. There was no photograph, not of the man and not of the acts that had made him, for a time, a notorious figure. These acts were noted in a single sentence, pointing out that he was the performance artist known as Falling Man.

She let the paper slip to the floor and turned off the light. She lay in bed, head propped on a couple of pillows. A car alarm began to sound down the street. She reached back for the pillow nearest her and dropped it on top of the newspaper and then lay back, breathing evenly, eyes still open. After a while she closed her eyes. Sleep was out there somewhere over the curve of the earth.

She waited for the car alarm to stop. When it stopped she turned on the light and got out of bed and went to the living room. There was a stack of old newspapers in a wicker basket. She looked for the five-day-old paper, which was the paper of the following day, but could not find it, whole or part, read or unread. She sat in the chair next to the basket waiting for something to happen or stop happening, a noise, a drone, an appliance, before she went to the computer in the next room.

The advanced search took no time. There he was, David Janiak, in pictures and print.

Dangling from the balcony of an apartment building on Central Park West.

Suspended from the roof of a loft building in the Williamsburg section of Brooklyn.

Dangling from the flies at Carnegie Hall during a concert, string section scattered.

Dangling over the East River from the Queensboro Bridge.

Sitting in the back seat of a police car.

Standing on the rail of a terrace.

Dangling from the bell tower of a church in the Bronx.

Dead at 39, apparently of natural causes.

He'd been arrested at various times for criminal trespass, reckless endangerment and disorderly conduct. He'd been beaten by a group of men outside a bar in Queens.

She clicked forward to the transcript of a panel discussion at the New School. Falling Man as Heartless Exhibitionist or Brave New Chronicler of the Age of Terror.

She read a few remarks, then stopped reading. She clicked forward to entries in Russian and other Slavic languages. She stared into the keyboard for a time.

Photographed being outfitted with a safety harness, an associate trying to shield him from the camera.

Photographed with bloody face in hotel lobby.

Dangling from parapet of tenement in Chinatown.

All his falls were headfirst, none announced in advance. The performance pieces were not designed to be recorded by a photographer. Those pictures that exist were taken by people who happened to be at the site or by a professional alerted to the event by a passerby.

He studied acting and dramaturgy at the Institute for Advanced Theatre Training in Cambridge, Massachusetts. His training included a three-month residency at the Moscow Art Theatre School.

Dead at 39. No sign of foul play. Suffered from a heart ailment and high blood pressure.

He worked without pulleys, cables or wires. Safety harness only. And no bungee cord to absorb the shock of longer falls. Just an arrangement of straps under the dress shirt and blue suit with one strand emerging from a trouser leg and extending back to a secure structure at the top of the fall.

Most charges dismissed. Fines and warnings issued.

She came across another burst of foreign languages, many words decorated with acute accents, circumflexes and other marks whose names she couldn't think of.

She looked into the screen waiting for a sound in the street, car brakes, car alarm, that would get her out of the room and back into bed.

His brother, Roman Janiak, a software engineer, assisted with most jumps, becoming visible to onlookers only when it was unavoidable. Plans for a final fall, according to him, did not include a safety harness.

She thought it could be the name of a trump card in a tarot deck, Falling Man, name in gothic type, the figure twisting down in a stormy night sky.

There is some dispute over the issue of the position he assumed during the fall, the position he maintained in his suspended state. Was this position intended to reflect the body posture of a particular man who was photographed falling from the north tower of the World Trade Center, headfirst, arms at his sides, one leg bent, a man set forever in free fall against the looming background of the column panels in the tower?

Free fall is the fall of a body within the atmosphere without a drag-producing device such as a parachute. It is the ideal falling motion of a body that is subject only to the earth's gravitational field.

She did not read further but knew at once which photograph the account referred to. It hit her hard when she first saw it, the day after, in the newspaper. The man headlong, the towers behind him. The mass of the towers filled the frame of the picture. The man falling, the towers contiguous, she thought, behind him. The enormous soaring lines, the vertical column stripes. The man with blood on his shirt, she thought, or burn

221

marks, and the effect of the columns behind him, the composition, she thought, darker stripes for the nearer tower, the north, lighter for the other, and the mass, the immensity of it, and the man set almost precisely between the rows of darker and lighter stripes. Headlong, free fall, she thought, and this picture burned a hole in her mind and heart, dear God, he was a falling angel and his beauty was horrific.

She clicked forward and there was the picture. She looked away, into the keyboard. It is the ideal falling motion of a body.

The preliminary finding is death from natural causes, pending an autopsy and toxicological report. Suffered from chronic depression due to a spinal condition.

If this photograph was an element in his performances he said nothing about it when questioned by reporters after one of his arrests. He said nothing when asked whether anyone close to him had been lost in the attacks. He had no comments to make to the media on any subject.

Suspended from the railing of a roof garden in Tribeca.

Dangling from a footbridge over the FDR Drive.

MAYOR SAYS FALL MAN MORONIC.

He turned down an invitation to fall from the upper reaches of the Guggenheim Museum at scheduled intervals over a three-week period. He turned down invitations to speak at the Japan Society, the New York Public Library and cultural organizations in Europe.

His falls were said to be painful and highly dangerous due to the rudimentary equipment he used.

His body was discovered by his brother, Roman Janiak, a software engineer. The Saginaw County medical examiner's office reports this was an apparent coronary event, tests pending.

His training included formal classes six days a week in both Cambridge and Moscow. Graduating actors gave a showcase presentation in New York for casting directors, artistic directors, agents and others. David Janiak, as a Brechtian dwarf, assaulted another actor, seemingly trying to rip the man's tongue out of his mouth during what was supposed to be a structured improvisation.

She clicked forward. She tried to connect this man to the moment when she'd stood beneath the elevated tracks, nearly three years ago, watching someone prepare to fall from a maintenance platform as the train went past. There were no photographs of that fall. She was the photograph, the photosensitive surface. That nameless body coming down, this was hers to record and absorb.

Early in 2003 he began to reduce the number of performances and tended to appear only in remote parts of the city. Then the performances stopped.

He injured his back so badly in one of the falls that he had to be hospitalized. Police arrested him at the hospital for obstructing vehicular traffic and creating a hazardous or physically offensive condition.

Plans for his final jump at some unforeseen future time did not include a harness, according to his brother Roman Janiak, 44, who spoke to a reporter shortly after he identified the body.

Students at the Institute create their own movement vocabulary and maintenance program to follow throughout their careers. Study includes psychophysical exercises, Meyerhold's biomechanics, Grotowski training, Vakhtangov's plasticity training, individual and partner acrobatics, classical and historical dance, style and genre explorations, Dalcroze eurythmics, impulse work, slow motion, fencing, armed and unarmed stage combat.

It is not immediately known what brought David Janiak to a motel outside the small town more than five hundred miles from the site of the World Trade Center.

She looked into the keyboard. The man eluded her. All she knew was what she'd seen and felt that day near the schoolyard, a boy bouncing a basketball and a teacher with a whistle on a string. She could believe she knew these people, and all the others she'd seen and heard that afternoon, but not the man who'd stood above her, detailed and looming.

She went to sleep finally on her husband's side of the bed.

14

There were rare moments between hands when he sat and listened to the sounds around him. It surprised him every time to find what an effort it takes to hear what is always there. The chips were there. Behind the ambient noise and stray voices, there was the sound of tossed chips, raked chips, forty or fifty tables of people stacking chips, fingers reading and counting, balancing the stacks, clay chips with smooth edges, rubbing, sliding, clicking, days and nights of distant hiss, like insect friction.

He was fitting into something that was made to his shape. He was never more himself than in these rooms, with a dealer crying out a vacancy at table seventeen. He was looking at pocket tens, waiting for the turn. These were the times when there was nothing outside, no flash of history or memory that he might unknowingly summon in the routine run of cards.

He walked down the wide aisle hearing the mutter of stickmen at the dice tables, a shout now and then from the sports book. Sometimes a hotel guest wheeling a suitcase wandered through, looking lost in Swaziland. In the off-hours he talked to dealers at empty blackjack tables, always the women, waiting in some zone of purged sensation. He might play a while, sitting and talking, making a point of not getting interested in the woman herself, just her conversation, fragments of life outside, her car trouble, her daughter Nadia's riding lessons. He was one of them in a way, casino staff, passing some forgettable social moments before the action starts again.

It would all go flat at the end of the night, win or lose, but that was part of the process, the turn card, the river card, the blinking woman. Days fade, nights drag on, check-and-raise, wake-and-sleep. The blinking woman was gone one day and that was the end of her. She was stale air. He could not place her elsewhere, at a bus stop, in a mall, and saw no point in trying.

He wondered if he was becoming a self-operating mechanism, like a humanoid robot that understands two hundred voice commands, far-seeing, touch-sensitive but totally, rigidly controllable.

He's estimating medium-ace across the table, the man in mirrored sunglasses.

Or a robot dog with infrared sensors and a pause button, subject to seventy-five voice commands.

Raise before the flop. Hit early and hard.

There was no fitness center in his hotel. He found a gym not far away and worked out when there was time. No one used the rowing machine. He half hated the thing, it made him angry, but he felt the intensity of the workout, the need to pull and strain, set his body against a sleek dumb punishing piece of steel and cable.

He rented a car and took a drive in the desert, starting back after dark and then climbing a rise and leveling out. It took him a moment to understand what he was looking at, many miles ahead, the city floating on the night, a feverish sprawl of light so quick and inexplicable it seemed a kind of delirium. He wondered why he'd never thought of himself in the middle of such a thing, living there more or less. He lived in rooms, that's why. He lived and worked in this room and that. He moved only marginally, room to room. He took a taxi to and from the downtown street where his hotel was located, a place without floor mosaics and heated towel racks, and he hadn't known until now, looking at that vast band of trembling desert neon, how strange a life he was living. But only from here, out away from it. In the thing itself, down close, in the tight eyes around the table, there was nothing that was not normal.

He was avoiding Terry Cheng. He didn't want to talk to him, or listen, or watch his cigarette burn down.

The lucky jack did not fall.

He didn't listen to what was said around him, the incidental bounce of dialogue, player to player. A fresh deck rose to the tabletop. He was gutted by fatigue at times, in a near feral state, eyes sweeping the table before the cards were dealt.

He used to think about Florence Givens every day. He still did, most days, today, in a taxi, staring at a billboard. He'd never called. He'd never thought of crossing the park again to see her, talk a while, find out how she was doing. He'd thought of it in a remote way, like landscape, like thinking of going back to the house where you grew up and walking along the back lanes and across the high meadow, the kind of thing you know you'll never do.

It was finally who he was that counted, not luck or naked skill. It was strength of mind, mental edge, but not just that. There was something harder to name, a narrowness of need or wish, or how a man's character determines his line of sight. These things would make him win but not too much, not winnings of such proportions that he'd slip into someone else's skin.

The dwarf is back, Carlo, and he is happy to see this, watching the man take a seat two tables away. But he doesn't look around the room for a sign of Terry Cheng so they might trade wry smiles.

Men in stylized yawns with arms raised, men staring into dead space.

Terry might be in Santa Fe or Sydney or Dallas. Terry might be in his room dead. It took Terry two weeks to understand that the fixture on the wall at one end of the long room, marked SHEER and BULK, was designed to operate the curtains at the other end of the room, to open and close the sheer inner curtain or the bulky outer. Terry had tried to open the curtains once by hand and then realized it didn't matter, open or closed. There was nothing out there he needed to know.

He'd never told Lianne about the walks across the park. His experience with Florence was brief, maybe four or five encounters over a period of fifteen days. Is that possible, only that? He tried counting the times, sitting in a taxi at a stoplight, staring at a billboard. It all ran together now, with only the faint grain of something felt and held. He saw her in the tower as she'd described it, in forced march down the stairwell, and thought he saw himself at times, in split instants, unshaped, a false memory or too warped and fleeting to be false.

The money mattered but not so much. The game mattered, the touch of felt beneath the hands, the way the dealer burnt one card, dealt the next. He wasn't playing for the money. He was playing for the chips. The value of each chip had only hazy meaning. It was the disk itself that mattered, the color itself. There was the laughing man at the far end of the room. There was the fact that they would all be dead one day. He wanted to rake in chips and stack them. The game mattered, the stacking of chips, the eye count, the play and dance of hand and eye. He was identical with these things.

He set the resistance level way up. He stroked hard, arms and legs but mostly legs, trying not to collapse his shoulders, hating every stroke. Sometimes there was no one else in the place, maybe somebody on a treadmill watching TV. He always used the rowing machine. He rowed and showered and the showers smelled of mildew. He stopped going after a while but then went back, setting the level higher still, wondering only once why this was a thing he had to do.

He was looking at five-deuce off-suit. He thought for a moment he might get up and leave. He thought he might walk out and get the first plane, pack and go, get a window seat and lower the shade and fall asleep. He folded his cards and sat back. By the time a fresh deck floated up he was ready to play again.

Forty tables, nine players a table, others waiting at the rail, screens high on three walls showing soccer and baseball, strictly atmospheric.

SHEER and BULK.

He didn't want to listen to Terry Cheng at his conversational ease, in his new persona, chatting away by the blue waterfall, three years after the planes.

Older men with chapped faces, eyelids drawn down. Would he know them if he saw them in a diner, eating breakfast at the next table? Long lifetimes of spare motion, sparer words, call the bet, see the raise, two or three such faces every day, men nearly unnoticeable. But they gave the game a niche in time, in the lore of poker face and dead man's hand, and a breath of self-esteem.

The waterfall was blue now, or possibly always was, or this was another waterfall or another hotel.

You have to break through the structure of your own stonework habit just to make yourself listen. There it is, the clink of chips, the toss and scatter, players and dealers, mass and stack, a light ringing sound so native to the occasion it lies outside the aural surround, in its own current of air, and no one hears it but you.

Here's Terry slouching down a side aisle at three a.m. and

they barely share a glance and Terry Cheng says, "Have to get back to my coffin by sunup."

The woman from wherever she's from, in the black leather cap, Bangkok or Singapore or L.A. She wears the cap slightly tilted and he knows they're all so neutralized by the steady throb of call and fold that there's very little happening, table-wide, in the popular art of fantasy fuck.

One night he sat in his room doing the old exercises, the old rehab program, bend of the wrist toward the floor, bend of the wrist toward the ceiling. Room service ended at midnight. Mid-night TV showed soft-core films with naked women and penis-less men. He was not lost or bored or crazy. Thursday tournament started at three, sign-ups at noon. Friday tournament started at noon, sign-ups at nine.

He was becoming the air he breathed. He moved in a tide of noise and talk made to his shape. The look under the thumb at ace-queen. Along the aisles, roulette wheels clicking. He sat in the sports book unaware of scores or odds or point spreads. He watched the miniskirted women serving drinks. Out on the Strip a dead and heavy heat. He folded eight or nine hands in a row. He stood in the sportswear shop wondering what he might buy for the kid. There were no days or times except for the tournament schedule. He wasn't making enough money to jus-tify this life on a practical basis. But there was no such need. There should have been but wasn't and that was the point. The point was one of invalidation. Nothing else pertained. Only this had binding force. He folded six more hands, then went all-in. Make them bleed. Make them spill their precious losers' blood.

These were the days after and now the years, a thousand heaving dreams, the trapped man, the fixed limbs, the dream of paralysis, the gasping man, the dream of asphyxiation, the dream of helplessness.

A fresh deck rose to the tabletop.

Fortune favors the brave. He didn't know the Latin original of the old adage and this was a shame. This is what he'd always lacked, that edge of unexpected learning.

She was only a girl, always a daughter, and her father was drinking a Tanqueray martini. He'd let her add a twist of lemon, giving her comically detailed instructions. Human existence, that was his subject this evening, on the deck of somebody's beat-up house in Nantucket. Five adults, the girl on the fringes. Human existence had to have a deeper source than our own dank fluids. Dank or rank. There had to be a force behind it, a principal being who was and is and ever shall be. She loved the sound of that, like chanted verse, and thought of it now, alone, over coffee and toast, and something else as well, the existence that hummed in the words themselves, was and is, and how the chill wind died at nightfall.

People were reading the Koran. She knew of three people doing this. She'd talked to two and knew of another. They'd bought English-language editions of the Koran and were trying earnestly to learn something, find something that might help them think more deeply into the question of Islam. She didn't know whether they were persisting in the effort. She could imagine herself doing this, the determined action that floats into empty gesture. But maybe they were persisting. They were serious people perhaps. She knew two of them but not well. One, a doctor, recited the first line of the Koran in his office.

This Book is not to be doubted.

She doubted things, she had her doubts. She took a long walk one day, uptown, to East Harlem. She missed her group, the laughter and cross talk, but knew all along this wasn't just a

231

walk, a matter of old times and places. She thought of the res-
olute hush that fell over the room when members took up pens
and began to write, oblivious to the clamor around them, rap
singers down the hall, barely school age, polishing their lyrics, or
workers drilling and hammering on the floor above. She was
here to look for something, a church, near the community center,
Catholic, she thought, and it may have been the church that
Rosellen S. used to go to. She wasn't sure but thought it might
be, made it be, said it was. She missed the faces. Your face is your
life, her mother said. She missed the forthright voices that began
to warp and fade, lives that dwindled into whisper.

She had normal morphology. She loved that word. But
what's inside the form and structure? This mind and soul, hers
and everyone's, keep dreaming toward something unreachable.
Does this mean there's something there, at the limits of matter
and energy, a force responsible in some way for the very nature,
the vibrancy of our lives from the mind out, the mind in little
pigeon blinks that extend the plane of being, out beyond logic
and intuition.

She wanted to disbelieve. She was an infidel in current
geopolitical parlance. She remembered how her father, how
Jack's face went bright and hot, appearing to buzz with electric
current after a day in the sun. Look around us, out there, up
there, ocean, sky, night, and she thought about this, over coffee
and toast, how he believed that God infused time and space with
pure being, made stars give light. Jack was an architect, an artist,
a sad man, she thought, for much of his life, and it was the kind
of sadness that yearns for something intangible and vast, the one
solace that might dissolve his paltry misfortune.

But this was crap, wasn't it, night skies and divinely inspired
stars. A star makes its own light. The sun is a star. She thought of
Justin night before last, singing his homework. This meant he

was bored, alone, in his room, making up monotone songs of addition and subtraction, presidents and vice-presidents.

Others were reading the Koran, she was going to church. She took a taxi uptown, weekdays, two or three times a week, and sat in the nearly empty church, Rosellen's church. She followed others when they stood and knelt and she watched the priest celebrate the mass, bread and wine, body and blood. She didn't believe this, the transubstantiation, but believed something, half fearing it would take her over.

She ran along the river, early light, before the kid was awake. She thought of training for the marathon, not this year's but next, the pain and rigor of it, long-distance running as spiritual effort.

She thought of Keith with a call girl in his room, having automated teller sex.

After mass she tried to hunt down a taxi. Taxis were scarce here and the bus took forever and she wasn't ready yet to take the subway.

This Book is not to be doubted.

She was stuck with her doubts but liked sitting in church. She went early, before mass began, to be alone for a while, to feel the calm that marks a presence outside the nonstop riffs of the waking mind. It was not something godlike she felt but only a sense of others. Others bring us closer. Church brings us closer. What did she feel here? She felt the dead, hers and unknown others. This is what she'd always felt in churches, great bloated cathedrals in Europe, a small poor parish church such as this one. She felt the dead in the walls, over decades and centuries. There was no dispiriting chill in this. It was a comfort, feeling their presence, the dead she'd loved and all the faceless others who'd filled a thousand churches. They brought intimacy and ease, the human ruins that lie in crypts and vaults or buried in churchyard plots. She sat and waited. Soon someone would enter and walk past her into the nave. She was always the first, always seated toward the rear, breathing the dead in candlewax and incense.

She thought of Keith and then he called. He said he'd be able to get home for a few days in a week or so and she said okay, good.

She saw the gray that was beginning to seep into her hair at the scalp. She would not stain it away. God, she thought. What does it mean to say that word? Are you born with God? If you never hear the word or observe the ritual, do you feel the breath alive inside you, in brain waves or pounding heart?

Her mother had a mane of white hair at the end, the body slowly broken, haunted by strokes, blood in the eyes. She was drifting into spirit life. She was a spirit woman now, barely able to make a sound that might pass for a word. She lay shrunken in bed, all that was left of her framed by the long straight hair, frosted white in sunlight, beautiful and otherworldly.

She sat in the empty church waiting for the pregnant woman to enter or maybe the old man who always nodded to her. One woman, then the other, or one woman and then the man. They'd established a pattern, these three, or nearly so, and then others entered and the mass began.

But isn't it the world itself that brings you to God? Beauty, grief, terror, the empty desert, the Bach cantatas. Others bring you closer, church brings you closer, the stained glass windows of a church, the pigments inherent in the glass, the metallic oxides fused onto the glass, God in clay and stone, or was she babbling to herself to pass the time?

She walked home from church when there was time but otherwise tried to find a cab, tried to talk to the driver, who was in the twelfth hour of his shift and wanted only to finish without dying.

She stayed away from the subway, still, and never stopped noticing the concrete bulwarks outside train stations and other possible targets.

She ran early mornings and came home and stripped and showered. God would consume her. God would de-create her and she was too small and tame to resist. That's why she was resisting now. Because think about it. Because once you believe such a thing, God is, then how can you escape, how survive the power of it, is and was and ever shall be.

He sat alongside the table, facing the dusty window. He placed his left forearm along the near edge of the table, hand dangling from the adjoining edge. This was the tenth day of twice-a-day, the wrist extensions, the ulnar deviations. He counted the days, the times per day.

There was no problem with the wrist. The wrist was fine. But he sat in his hotel room, facing the window, hand curled into a gentle fist, thumb up in certain setups. He recalled phrases from the instruction sheet and recited them quietly, working on the hand shapes, the bend of the wrist toward the floor, the bend of the wrist toward the ceiling. He used the uninvolved hand to apply pressure to the involved hand.

He sat in deep concentration. He recalled the setups, every one, and the number of seconds for each, and the number of repetitions. With your palm down, bend your wrist toward the floor. With your forearm resting sideways, bend your wrist toward the floor. He did the wrist flexions, the radial deviations.

Mornings without fail, every night when he returned. He looked into the dusty glass, reciting fragments from the instruction sheet. Hold to a count of five. Repeat ten times. He did the full program every time, hand raised, forearm flat, hand down, forearm sideways, slowing the pace just slightly, day to night and then again the following day, drawing it out, making it last. He counted the seconds, he counted the repetitions.

There were nine people at mass today. She watched them stand, sit and kneel and she did what they did but failed to respond as they did when the priest recited lines from the liturgy.

She thought that the hovering possible presence of God was the thing that created loneliness and doubt in the soul and she also thought that God was the thing, the entity existing outside space and time that resolved this doubt in the tonal power of a word, a voice.

God is the voice that says, "I am not here."

She was arguing with herself but it wasn't argument, just the noise the brain makes.

She had normal morphology. Then one late night, undressing, she yanked a clean green T-shirt over her head and it wasn't sweat she smelled or maybe just a faint trace but not the sour reek of the morning run. It was just her, the body through and through. It was the body and everything it carried, inside and out, identity and memory and human heat. It wasn't even something she smelled so much as knew. It was something she'd always known. The child was in it, the girl who wanted to be other people, and obscure things she could not name. It was a small moment, already passing, the kind of moment that is always only seconds from forgetting.

She was ready to be alone, in reliable calm, she and the kid, the way they were before the planes appeared that day, silver crossing blue.

The aircraft was secured now and he sat in the jump seat across from the forward galley, keeping watch. He was either supposed to keep watch here, outside the cockpit, or to patrol the aisle, box cutter in hand. He was not confused, only catching a breath, taking a moment. This is when he felt a sensation high on his arm, the thin wincing pain of slit skin.

He sat facing a bulkhead, with the toilet behind him, first-class only.

The air was thick with the Mace he'd sprayed and there was somebody's blood, his blood, draining through the cuff of his long-sleeved shirt. It was his blood. He didn't look for the source of the wound but saw more blood beginning to show through the sleeve up toward the shoulder. He thought that maybe the pain had been there earlier but he was only now remembering to feel it. He didn't know where the box cutter was.

If other things were normal, in his understanding of the plan, the aircraft was headed toward the Hudson corridor. This was the phrase he'd heard from Amir many times. There was no window he might look through without getting out of the seat and he felt no need to do that.

He had his cell phone on vibrate.

Everything was still. There was no sensation of flight. He

heard noise but felt no motion and the noise was the kind that overtakes everything and seems completely natural, all the engines and systems that become the air itself.

Forget the world. Be unmindful of the thing called the world.

All of life's lost time is over now.

This is your long wish, to die with your brothers.

His breath came in short bursts. His eyes were burning. When he looked left, partway, he could see an empty seat in the first-class cabin, on the aisle. Straight ahead, the bulkhead. But there was a view, there was a scene of clear imagining out the back of his head.

He didn't know how he'd been cut. He'd been cut by one of his brothers, how else, accidentally, in the struggle, and he welcomed the blood but not the pain, which was becoming hard to bear. Then he thought of something he'd long forgotten. He thought of the Shia boys on the battlefield in the Shatt al Arab. He saw them coming out of trenches and redoubts and running across the mudflats toward enemy positions, mouths open in mortal cry. He took strength from this, seeing them cut down in waves by machine guns, boys in the hundreds, then the thousands, suicide brigades, wearing red bandannas around their necks and plastic keys underneath, to open the door to paradise.

Recite the sacred words.

Pull your clothes tightly about you.

Fix your gaze.

Carry your soul in your hand.

He believed he could see straight into the towers even though his back was to them. He didn't know the aircraft's location but believed he could see straight out the back of his head and through the steel and aluminum of the aircraft and into the long silhouettes, the shapes, the forms, the figures coming closer, the material things.

The pious ancestors had pulled their clothes tightly about them before battle. They were the ones who named the way. How could any death be better?

Every sin of your life is forgiven in the seconds to come.

There is nothing between you and eternal life in the seconds to come.

You are wishing for death and now it is here in the seconds to come.

He began to vibrate. He wasn't sure whether it was the motion of the plane or only himself. He rocked in his seat, in pain. He heard sounds from somewhere in the cabin. The pain was worse now. He heard voices, excited cries from the cabin or the cockpit, he wasn't sure. Something fell off the counter in the galley.

He fastened his seatbelt.

A bottle fell off the counter in the galley, on the other side of the aisle, and he watched it roll this way and that, a water bottle, empty, making an arc one way and rolling back the other, and he watched it spin more quickly and then skitter across the floor an instant before the aircraft struck the tower, heat, then fuel, then fire, and a blast wave passed through the structure that sent Keith Neudecker out of his chair and into a wall. He found himself walking into a wall. He didn't drop the telephone until he hit the wall. The floor began to slide beneath him and he lost his balance and eased along the wall to the floor.

He saw a chair bounce down the corridor in slow motion. He thought he saw the ceiling begin to ripple, lift and ripple. He put his arms over his head and sat knees up, face wedged between them. He was aware of vast movement and other things, smaller, unseen, objects drifting and skidding, and sounds that weren't one thing or another but only sound, a shift in the basic arrangement of parts and elements.

The movement was beneath him and then all around him, massive, something undreamed. It was the tower lurching. He understood this now. The tower began a long sway left and he raised his head. He took his head out of his knees to listen. He tried to be absolutely still and tried to breathe and tried to listen. Out past the office door he thought he saw a man on his knees in the first pale wave of smoke and dust, a figure deep in concentration, head up, jacket halfway off, dangling from one shoulder.

In time he felt the tower stop leaning. The lean felt forever and impossible and he sat and listened and after a while the tower began to roll slowly back. He didn't know where the phone was but he could hear a voice on the other end, still there, somewhere. He saw the ceiling begin to ripple. The stink of something familiar was everywhere but he didn't know what it was.

When the tower swung finally back to vertical he pushed himself off the floor and moved to the doorway. The ceiling at the far end of the hall moaned and opened. The stress was audible and then it opened, objects coming down, panels and wallboard. Plaster dust filled the area and there were voices along the hall. He was losing things as they happened. He felt things come and go.

The man was still there, kneeling in the doorway of the office opposite, thinking hard about something, blood showing through his shirt. He was a client or consulting attorney and Keith knew him slightly and they exchanged a look. No telling what it meant, this look. There were people calling along the hall. He took his jacket off the door. He reached behind the door and took his jacket from the hook, not sure why he was doing this but not feeling stupid about it, forgetting to feel stupid.

He went down the hall, putting on the jacket. There were people moving toward the exits, in the other direction, moving, coughing, helping others. They stepped over debris, faces showing stark urgency. This was the knowledge in every face, the distance they had to cover to street level. They spoke to him, one or two, and he nodded back or didn't. They spoke and looked. He was the guy who thought jackets were required, the guy going the wrong way.

The stink was fuel and he recognized it now, oozing down from floors above. He got to Rumsey's office at the end of the hall. He had to climb in. He climbed over chairs and strewn books and a filing cabinet on its side. He saw bare framework, truss bars, where the ceiling had been. Rumsey's coffee mug was shattered in his hand. He still held a fragment of the mug, his finger through the ring.

Only it didn't look like Rumsey. He sat in his chair, head to one side. He'd been hit by something large and hard when the ceiling caved or even before, in the first spasm. His face was pressed into his shoulder, some blood, not much.

Keith talked to him.

He squatted alongside and took his arm and looked at the man, talking to him. Something came trickling from the corner of Rumsey's mouth, like bile. What's bile look like? He saw the mark on his head, an indentation, a gouge mark, deep, exposing raw tissue and nerve.

The office was small and makeshift, a cubicle wedged into a corner, with a limited view of morning sky. He felt the dead nearby. He sensed this, in the hanging dust.

He watched the man breathe. He was breathing. He looked like someone paralyzed for life, born this way, head twisted into his shoulder, living in a chair day and night.

There was fire up there somewhere, fuel burning, smoke

blowing out of a ventilation duct, then smoke outside the window, crawling down the surface of the building.

He unbent Rumsey's index finger and removed the broken mug.

He got to his feet and looked at him. He talked to him. He told him he could not wheel him out in the chair, wheels or not, because debris everywhere, he talked quickly, debris blocking door and hall, talking quickly to get himself to think in like manner.

Things began to fall, one thing and then another, things singly at first, coming down out of the gap in the ceiling, and he tried lifting Rumsey out of the chair. Then something outside, going past the window. Something went past the window, then he saw it. First it went and was gone and then he saw it and had to stand a moment staring out at nothing, holding Rumsey under the arms.

He could not stop seeing it, twenty feet away, an instant of something sideways, going past the window, white shirt, hand up, falling before he saw it. Debris in clusters came down now. There were echoes sounding down the floors and wires snapping at his face and white powder everywhere. He stood through it, holding Rumsey. The glass partition shattered. Something came down and there was a noise and then the glass shivered and broke and then the wall gave way behind him.

It took some time to push himself up and out. His face felt like a hundred pinpoint fires and it was hard to breathe. He found Rumsey in the smoke and dust, facedown in the rubble and bleeding badly. He tried to lift him and turn him and found he couldn't use his left hand but was able to turn him partly.

He wanted to raise him onto his shoulder, using his left forearm to help guide the upper body while he grabbed the belt with his right hand and tried to snatch and lift.

He began to lift, his face warm with the blood on Rumsey's shirt, blood and dust. The man jumped in his grip. There was a noise in his throat, abrupt, a half second, half gasp, and then blood from somewhere, floating, and Keith turned away, hand still clutching the man's belt. He waited, trying to breathe. He looked at Rumsey, who'd fallen away from him, upper body lax, face barely belonging. The whole business of being Rumsey was in shambles now. Keith held tight to the belt buckle. He stood and looked at him and the man opened his eyes and died.

This is when he wondered what was happening here.

Paper was flying down the hallway, rattling in a wind that seemed to wash down from above.

There were dead, faintly seen, in offices to either side.

He climbed out over a fallen wall and made his way slowly toward the voices.

In the stairwell, in near dark, a woman carried a small tricycle tight to her chest, a thing for a three-year-old, handlebars framing her ribs.

They walked down, thousands, and he was in there with them. He walked in a long sleep, one step and then the next.

There was water running somewhere and voices in an odd distance, coming from another stairwell or an elevator bank, out in the dark somewhere.

It was hot and crowded and the pain in his face seemed to shrink his head. He thought his eyes and mouth were sinking into his skin.

Things came back to him in hazy visions, like half an eye staring. These were moments he'd lost as they were happening and he had to stop walking in order to stop seeing them. He stood looking into nothing. The woman with the tricycle, along-side, spoke to him, going past.

He smelled something dismal and understood it was him, things sticking to his skin, dust particles, smoke, some kind of oily grit on his face and hands mixing with the body slop, paste-like, with the blood and saliva and cold sweat, and it was himself he smelled, and Rumsey.

The size of it, the sheer physical dimensions, and he saw himself in it, the mass and scale, and the way the thing swayed, the slow and ghostly lean.

Someone took his arm and led him forward for a few steps and then he walked on his own, in his sleep, and for an instant he saw it again, going past the window, and this time he thought it was Rumsey. He confused it with Rumsey, the man falling sideways, arm out and up, like pointed up, like why am I here instead of there.

They had to wait at times, long stalled moments, and he looked straight ahead. When the line moved again he took a step down and then another. They talked to him several times, different people, and when this happened he closed his eyes, maybe because it meant he didn't have to reply.

There was a man on the landing ahead, old man, smallish, sitting in shadow, knees up, resting. Some people spoke and he nodded his head okay, he waved them on nodding.

There was a woman's shoe nearby, upside down. There was a briefcase on its side and the man had to lean to reach it. He extended a hand and pushed it with some effort toward the advancing line.

He said, "I don't know what I'm supposed to do with this. She fell and left it."

People didn't hear this or retain it or want to and they

moved past, Keith moved past, the line beginning to wind down toward an area of some light.

It did not seem forever to him, the passage down. He had no sense of pace or rate. There was a glow stripe on the stairs that he hadn't seen before and someone praying back in the line somewhere, in Spanish.

A man came up, moving quickly, in a hard hat, and they cleared a space, and then there were firemen, in full bulk, and they cleared a space.

Rumsey was the one in the chair. He understood that now. He had set him back down in the chair and they would find him and bring him down, and others.

There were voices up behind him, back on the stairs, one and then another in near echo, fugue voices, song voices in the rhythms of natural speech.

This goes down.

This goes down.

Pass it down.

He stopped again, second time or third, and people pushed around him and looked at him and told him to move. A woman took his arm to help and he didn't move and she went on.

Pass it down.

This goes down.

This goes down.

The briefcase came down and around the stairwell, hand to hand, somebody left this, somebody lost this, this goes down, and he stood looking straight ahead and when the briefcase came to him, he reached his right hand across his body to take it, blankly, and then started down the stairs again.

There were long waits and others not so long and in time they were led down to the concourse level, beneath the plaza, and they moved past empty shops, locked shops, and they were running now, some of them, with water pouring in from somewhere. They came out onto the street, looking back, both towers burning, and soon they heard a high drumming rumble and saw smoke rolling down from the top of one tower, billowing out and down, methodically, floor to floor, and the tower falling, the south tower diving into the smoke, and they were running again.

The windblast sent people to the ground. A thunderhead of smoke and ash came moving toward them. The light drained dead away, bright day gone. They ran and fell and tried to get up, men with toweled heads, a woman blinded by debris, a woman calling someone's name. The only light was vestigial now, the light of what comes after, carried in the residue of smashed matter, in the ash ruins of what was various and human, hovering in the air above.

He took one step and then the next, smoke blowing over him. He felt rubble underfoot and there was motion everywhere, people running, things flying past. He walked by the Easy Park sign, the Breakfast Special and Three Suits Cheap, and they went running past, losing shoes and money. He saw a woman with her hand in the air, like running to catch a bus.

He went past a line of fire trucks and they stood empty now, headlights flashing. He could not find himself in the things he saw and heard. Two men ran by with a stretcher, someone facedown, smoke seeping out of his hair and clothes. He watched them move into the stunned distance. That's where everything was, all around him, falling away, street signs, people, things he could not name.

Then he saw a shirt come down out of the sky. He walked and saw it fall, arms waving like nothing in this life.

picador.com

blog
videos
interviews
extracts